T0209260

She was raised to be beautiful, nothing more. And then the rules changed…

In icy Dasnaria, rival realm to the Twelve Kingdoms, a woman's role is to give pleasure, produce heirs, and question nothing. But a plot to overthrow the emperor depends on the fate of his eldest daughter. And the treachery at its heart will change more than one carefully limited life…

THE GILDED CAGE

Princess Jenna has been raised in supreme luxury—and ignorance. Within the sweet-scented, golden confines of the palace seraglio, she's never seen the sun, or a man, or even learned her numbers. But she's been schooled enough in the paths to a woman's power. When her betrothal is announced, she's ready to begin the machinations that her mother promises will take Jenna from ornament to queen.

But the man named as Jenna's husband is no innocent to be cozened or prince to charm. He's a monster in human form, and the horrors of life under his thumb are clear within moments of her wedding vows. If Jenna is to live, she must somehow break free—and for one born to a soft prison, the way to cold, hard freedom will be a dangerous path indeed…

Books by Jeffe Kennedy

The Master of the Opera

The Twelve Kingdoms:
The Mark of the Tala
The Tears of the Rose
The Talon of the Hawk

The Uncharted Realms:
The Pages of the Mind
The Edge of the Blade

The Lost Princess Chronicles
Prisoner of the Crown

Prisoner of the Crown

Jeffe Kennedy

REBEL BASE

REBEL BASE BOOKS
Kensington Publishing Corp.
www.kensingtonbooks.com

Rebel Base Books are published by
Kensington Publishing Corp. 119 West 40th Street New York, NY 10018

Special book excerpts or customized printings can also be created to fit
specific needs. For details, write or phone the office of the Kensington
Special Sales Manager:
Kensington Publishing Corp.
119 West 40th Street
New York, NY 10018
Attn. Special Sales Department. Phone: 1-800-221-2647.

First Electronic Edition: June 2018
eISBN-13: 978-1-63573-040-1
eISBN-10: 1-63573-040-6

First Print Edition: June 2018
ISBN-13: 978-1-63573-043-2
ISBN-10: 1-63573-043-0

Printed in the United States of America

To Kelly Robson, who inspires me regularly, and delights me daily

Acknowledgments

Much appreciation to my Santa Fe Critique Group, who read the initial pages and gave me feedback: Sage Walker, Eric Wolf, Ed Khmara, M.T. Reitan, and Jim Sorenson. Particular thanks to Jim, for a full read and excellent advice. You all have helped me see my writing in a different light.

Thanks and love to Margaret, for daily installments on the ongoing conversation and insights into everything. Also for the thoughtful critique of this manuscript—and in advance for discussion on book two.

A :**wave:** to all the folks in the Science Fiction and Fantasy Writers of America (SFWA) Slack chat room. Checking in with you all virtually makes my days that much brighter.

Flowers and chocolate to Sarah Younger, my wonderful agent, who nagged me to take this deal and turned things around for me in so many ways. Because of you I wrote Jenna's tale, and I'm glad for it.

Thanks to Tara Gavin, Rebecca Cremonese, and all the team at Rebel Base Books for all their hard work on this book.

As always, love and gratitude to David, who makes it all possible, in so many ways.

~ 1 ~

I grew up in paradise.

Tropically warm, lushly beautiful, replete with luxury, my childhood world was without flaw. My least whim was met with immediate indulgence, served instantly and with smiles of delight. I swam in crystal clear waters, then napped on silk. I chased gorgeously ornamental fish and birds, and enjoyed dozens of perfectly behaved pets of unusual coloring and pedigrees. My siblings and I spent our days in play, nothing ever asked or expected of us.

Until the day everything was demanded—and taken—from me.

Only then did I finally see our paradise for what it was, how deliberately designed to mold and shape us. A breeding ground for luxurious accessories. To create a work of art, you grow her in an environment of elegance and beauty. To make her soft and lusciously accommodating, you surround her with delicacies and everything delightful. And you don't educate her in anything but being pleasing.

Education leads to critical thinking, not a desirable trait in a princess of Dasnaria, thus I was protected from anything that might taint the virginity of my mind, as well as my body.

Because I'd understood so little of the world outside, when my time came to be plucked from the garden, when the snip of the shears severed me from all I'd known, the injury came as a shock so devastating that I had no ability to even understand what it meant, much less summon the will to resist and overcome. Which, I've also come to realize over time, was also a part of the deliberate design.

But I'm getting ahead of myself. Let me go back to the beginning.

I grew up in paradise.

And it was all you'd imagine paradise to be. A soft palace of lagoons and lush gardens, of silk bowers and laughter. With little else to do, our mothers and the other ladies played with us, games both simple and extravagantly layered. When we tired, we napped on the velvet soft grass of the banks of the pools, or on the silk pillows scattered everywhere. We'd sleep until we awoke, eat the tidbits served us by watchful servant girls, then play more.

Hestar and I had our own secret games and language. All the ladies called us the royal pair, as we were the emperor's firstborns and we'd been born less than a month apart.

My mother, first wife, the Empress Hulda, and the most highly ranked woman in the empire, spent much of her day at court. When she was home in the seraglio, she preferred to relax without noisy children to bother her. Hestar's mother, Jilliya, was second wife and kept getting pregnant, forever having and sometimes losing the babies. So, by unspoken agreement, we kept clear of her apartments, too. Something else I understood much later, that the miasma of misery has its own brand of contagion—and that those who fear contracting the deadly disease stay far away.

Saira, on the other hand, third wife and mother of our half-sister Inga, had a kindness and sweetness to her, so we kids often played in her apartments when we grew bored of games like climbing the palm trees to see who could pluck the most dates while a servant counted the time. Inga, along with my full brother, Kral, were the second oldest pair—the second-borns, also arriving in the same month, to my mother and Saira. Less than a year younger than Hestar and me, they completed our set of four. Our six other brothers and sisters played with us, too, but they were babies still, needing to be watched all the time. Whenever we could, the four of us ditched the babies, exploring the far corners of our world, then making hideouts where no one could find us.

Though, of course, when the least desire took our fancy, someone always appeared instantaneously to satisfy us. Another of the many illusions of my childhood.

Hestar and I, we had a cave we'd made under a clump of ferns. He'd stocked it with a box of sweetmeats and I'd stolen one of my mother's silk throws for a carpet. Embroidered with fabulous animals, it told tales of a world beyond our corner of paradise. We loved it best of all our purloined treasures, and made up stories about the scenes and creatures, giving them names and convoluted histories.

One day—the kind that stands out with crystalline clarity, each detail incised in my memory—we played as usual. Hestar had been mysteriously gone for a while the day before, or perhaps several days before or for several days in a row. That part fogs in with the timelessness of those days that never ended, but blended one into the next. What I remember is the elephant.

"And the miskagiggle flapped its face tail, saying nooo—"

"It's called an elephant," Hestar interrupted me.

"What is?"

"It's not a miskagiggle. It's an elephant, and the face tail is a trunk." Hestar beamed with pride at knowing something I didn't.

"You're making that up."

"No, I'm not! My tutor told me."

"What's that?"

"A teacher. My tutor is named Ser Llornsby."

"Is that where you went?" Hestar and Kral had been whisked off by servants, and no one would tell me or Inga where they were, just that we'd see them again soon.

Hestar's blue eyes went wide and he looked around to see if anyone was listening. "Want to know a secret?"

Oh, did I. Even then I understood that secrets were the carefully hoarded and counted currency of the seraglio. "Yes!"

We pulled the silk throw over our heads to make a tent. It was the usual grass beneath, so we didn't really need the carpet. Having it just made our hideaway more special—and the throw became a blanket, excellent for exchanging secrets.

"We went through the doors!" Hestar told me, whispering but much too loudly.

I hushed him. I didn't question how I knew, but this secret held power. Most of our secrets had been silly, frivolous things, like how Inga kept candied dates under her pillow. Or ones everyone already knew, like that Jilliya was pregnant again. With the unabashed enthusiasm of children, we absorbed all the murmured gossip and repeated it with equal relish. This, though—I recognized immediately how important it was.

No wonder no one would tell us where they'd gone. Children didn't go through the doors. Only my mother and some of the women. The rekjabrel and other servants, they went in and out all the time. But a lot of times they came back crying or hurt, so we understood the doors led to a terrible place. And yet Hestar had gone and returned, beaming.

"Was it terrible? Were you scared? Did Kral go, too?"

Hestar nodded, solemnly. "We were brave boys though. And it's not like here. There aren't the lagoons and it's not as warm. They took us to a library and we met Ser Llornsby. We looked at pictures and learned animal names."

I couldn't bring myself to ask what a library might be. I wanted to look at pictures and learn animal names. Though I didn't know the emotion to name it at the time, a jab of envy lanced through my heart. Hestar and I always had everything the same, only I had the better mother, because she was first wife. It wasn't fair that Hestar got to go through the doors and learn things without me. An elephant. I whispered the exotic word to myself.

"Elephants are huge and people ride on their backs, and the elephants carry things for them in their trunks." Hestar continued, full of smug pride. "Ser Llornsby is going to teach me everything I need to know to be emperor someday."

"Why do you get to be emperor? My mother is first wife. Yours is only second wife. Besides, I'm older."

Hestar wrinkled his nose at me. "Because you're a girl. Girls can't be emperor. Only empress."

That was true. It was the way of things. "Well then you can be emperor and I can be empress like Mother."

"All right!" Hestar grinned. "We'll rule the whole empire and have lots of elephants. Kral and Inga can be our servants."

For the rest of the day we played emperor and empress. Kral and Inga got mad and decided they would be emperor and empress, too, not listening when we said there could only be one of each and we were firstborn so they had to be our servants. They went off to play their own game, but we got Helva to be in our court, and also her little brothers, Leo and Loke. The boys were identical twins and liked any game they could play together. Baby Harlan could barely toddle, so he stayed with his nurse. Ban went off with Inga, of course, as he followed her everywhere, but her full brother, Mykal came to our side.

We didn't care, because our court was the biggest. Besides, everyone knew the emperor gets to pick his own empress, and Hestar already promised me I'd be first wife and I could pick his other wives, just like Mother did. Which meant Inga wouldn't get to be one. Maybe not Helva, either, though I told her she would be.

Mother didn't much care for Saira and Jilliya, so maybe I wouldn't have other wives at all. I didn't need them to be empress.

Playing emperor and empress turned out to be terribly fun. Hestar made me a crown of orchids and we took over one of the small eating salons, getting the servants to clear out the table and pillows, instead setting up two big chairs to be our thrones. His Imperial Majesty Emperor Einarr Konyngrr, our father, had a throne. So we'd heard. And we badgered one of the rekjabrel who'd served in the court to tell us what it looked like.

"Huge, Your Imperial Highnesses," she said, keeping her eyes averted. "It towers above, all platinum and crystal, so bright you can't look upon it. I can't say more."

"What about the Empress's throne?" I persisted.

"Just the one throne, Your Imperial Highness Princess Jenna."

"That can't be right," I told Hestar, when we let the rekjabrel go. "She must not have seen properly."

"We don't have platinum anyway," he replied.

So we decorated the two big chairs, which ended up taking a long time. They needed to be sparkling, which meant we needed jewels. Leo and Loke were good at persuading bangles off the ladies, but then didn't like to give them up. By the time we chased them down and got everything decorated, we had only a little time to have actual court. When my nurse, Kaia, came to get me for my bath, we made all the servants promise to leave everything as it was.

"Kaia?" I asked, splashing at the warmed milk water as she poured the jasmine rinse through my hair.

"Yes, Princess?"

"Have you seen an elephant?"

She laughed. "No, Princess. I've never heard of such a thing. Is this one of your games?"

"No—they're real. Their face-tails are called trunks."

"If you say so, Princess."

I fumed a little. How could I find out more about elephants when no one even believed they were real? "When do I get to go through the doors and look at pictures of animals and learn their names?"

Kaia dropped the pitcher of jasmine water, breaking it on the tiles. I would have scolded her for clumsiness, but she had such an odd look on her face that I stopped mid-word.

"Where have you heard of such a thing, Princess?" She had her head bowed, but with her scalp shorn, she couldn't hide her face. She'd gone white, her eyes squinched up like she hurt. Just like that time Mother accused her of drinking from her special teapot, and had Kaia lashed until she confessed. Kaia had cried and cried, not wanting to play with me for days afterward. But this time she didn't have any blood, so I didn't understand why she went all pale like that.

"Hestar got to go. And Kral, too, and he's younger. I want to go. I command you to take me tomorrow."

"Your Imperial Highness, I cannot."

"You will or I'll tell Mother."

"Up and out, Princess," she replied, dumping the shards into a waste bin, then holding out a towel. "We must address this with Her Imperial Majesty. You can ask her in person."

She dried me off, too briskly, and I almost reprimanded her, but she still looked so scared and I didn't want her to not play with me for days again.

"I already said goodnight to Mother." Mother didn't like to be disturbed after goodnights, and the prospect began to make me a little afraid, too.

Kaia wrapped my hair in a towel, then rubbed me all over with jasmine-scented unguent. She worked as thoroughly as always, but wouldn't answer any more questions, simply saying that I could ask my mother momentarily. She pulled my nightgown over my head and had me put on a robe, too, which wasn't usual. And we went with my hair still damp, not carefully combed dry before the fire while she told me stories.

I didn't want to miss my stories and I began to be afraid I'd said something terribly wrong. I'd known this was an important secret. How could I have been so careless? It was the elephant. "Let's not go see Mother," I said.

Kaia shook her head, pressing her lips together. "I apologize, Princess, but I'm afraid we must."

"I don't want to. Tell me my stories. My hair is still wet."

But she didn't bend, which scared me even more. Kaia always did what I told her. Almost always. She took my hand in a grip so firm it nearly hurt and practically dragged me to Mother's private salon. I resisted, and would have thrown a fit, but Mother wouldn't like that. An imperial princess gives commands in a firm and gentle voice, never shrill, and tears are unacceptable.

Still, when Kaia called out through the closed yellow silk curtains, and my mother snapped out a reply, I nearly did cry. And Kaia didn't relent in her grip, which made me think she was angry with me and Kaia was never angry, even when I refused to eat my supper and demanded dessert instead.

She parted the curtains and slipped me inside, kneeling beside me and bowing her head to the plush tapestried carpet. I lowered my eyes, too, though I didn't have to kneel.

"Well?" the empress demanded in a cold tone. "What is the meaning of this, child?"

"My humble apologies, Your Imperial Majesty," Kaia said, though Mother had clearly asked me. Her voice shook and her hand had gone all cold and sweaty. I yanked mine away and she let me. "Her Imperial Highness Princess Jenna has asked me questions I cannot answer. I thought it best to bring her to you immediately."

"It's not your responsibility to think," Mother replied. A hissing sound as she breathed in her relaxing smoke. "You are to keep the princess well groomed, as she most certainly is not at the moment. Your hair is wet, Jenna."

A tear slipped down my cheek, making me glad that I was to keep my eyes averted unless given permission. Maybe she wouldn't see. "I'm sorry, Mother," I whispered.

"As well you should be. Interrupting my quiet time. Going about like a rekjabrel with wild hair. Are you a princess of Dasnaria?"

"Yes, Your Imperial Majesty."

She hmphed in derision. "You don't look like one. What question did you ask to upset your nurse so?"

Kaia had gone silent, quaking on the carpet beside me. No help at all. I considered lying, saying Kaia had made it up. But Mother wouldn't believe that. Kaia would never so recklessly attract punishment. I happened to know she hadn't snuck the tea—one of the rekjabrel had taken it for her sister, but Kaia had never said.

"Jenna," Mother said, voice like ice. "Look at me."

I did, feeling defiant, for no good reason. Mother reclined on her pillows, her embroidered silk gown a river of blues over their ruby reds. Her unbound hair flowed over it all, a pale blond almost ivory, like mine. In contrast, her eyes looked black as ebony, darker even than the artful shadows outlining them. She'd removed most of her jewelry, wearing only the wedding bracelets that never came off. She held her glass pipe in her jeweled nails. The scarlet of her lip paint left a waxy mark on the end of it, scented smoke coiling from the bowl.

"Tears?" Her voice dripped contempt and disbelief. "What could you possibly have said to have your nurse in a puddle and an imperial princess in tears, simply in anticipation?"

"I didn't say anything!" I answered.

"Your nurse is lying then," the empress cooed. "I shall have to punish her."

Kaia let out this noise, like the one Inga's kitten had made when Ban kicked it. The ladies had taken it to a better home and Inga had cried for days until they gave her five new kittens just like it.

"I only asked about the elephants," I said, very quietly.

"Excuse me?" The arch of her darkened brows perfectly echoed her tone.

"Elephants!" I yelled at her, and burst into full-fledged sobbing. If you'd asked me then, what made me break all those rules, raising my voice, defying my mother, losing the composure expected of an imperial princess, firstborn daughter of Emperor Einarr, I likely could only have explained that I wanted to know about elephants so badly that it felt like a physical ache. Something extraordinary for a girl who'd rarely experienced pain of any sort.

Once I'd had a pet, an emerald lizard with bright yellow eyes. Its scales felt like cool water against my skin, and it would wrap its tail tightly around my wrist. I'd only had it a day when it bit me. Astonished by the bright pain, the blood flowing from my finger, I'd barely registered that I'd been hurt before the servants descended, wrapping the wound in bandages soaked in sweet smelling salve that took sensation away.

They also took the lizard away and wouldn't give it back, despite my demands and pleas. When the salve wore off, my finger throbbed. And when they took the bandages off, the skin around the bite had turned a fascinating purple and gray. They tried to keep me from looking, but I caught glimpses before they made it numb again, then wrapped it up and I couldn't see it anymore. I'd tap my finger against things, trying to feel it again. My finger and the lizard, both gone.

I felt like that, full of purple bruising and soft pain, as if I'd been bitten inside, and somehow numb on the outside. I wondered what might disappear this time.

"Elephants," my mother pronounced the word softly, almost in wonder. Then she laughed, not at all nicely. "Leave us," she snapped, making Kaia scurry backwards. "It's apparently time for me to have a conversation about life with my daughter."

~ 2 ~

"Elephants," my mother repeated once Kaia had fled entirely. Her scarlet mouth curved in a smile I didn't recognize. "I suppose Hestar and Kral told you about them."

I nodded, much easier—and safer—than giving details. She sighed and patted the pillows beside her, beckoning me to sit as I hadn't done for more than a year, not since I'd turned five and became a big girl, too old for nighttime cuddles. I might've minded more if Kral hadn't been ejected also—and him not even quite five at the time—because boys grow up faster than girls. And then Mother didn't have any more babies after us.

Tentatively, I settled into that space, wreathed in the muggy sweet opos smoke that reminded me of being little again. Mother transferred her pipe to her other hand, threading her nails through my damp hair. "You're growing up," she observed. "All of you are. And you are imperial princes and princesses. You have everything you could wish for."

"Yes, Mother, and I'm grateful," I replied, as I'd been taught.

"Yet you wish for more," she mused. "Why?"

I looked at my hands in my lap, my pretty robe a pale ghost against the rich colors of the empress's. "Hestar has more," I said.

"Ah. What did Jilliya's son tell you, hmm?" She had that cooing voice, the one that made me think of the silky scales and sharp teeth of the beautiful lizard that bit me.

"He and Kral went through the doors—to outside!" I risked a glance at her, her eyes so dark. "A tutor talked to them and showed them pictures of elephants. Hestar is learning to be emperor someday."

Mother drew on her pipe, a quiet rush of air, and she hmmd deep in her throat. "That is the way of things. They must go out while you may stay

in. Boys don't belong in the seraglio, not once they're old enough. It's time
for them to be weaned from the world of women, Hestar and Kral, while
you and Inga will stay with us. The world outside the doors is a harsh and
dangerous place. It's a privilege to be allowed to stay."

"It is?" It didn't seem that way. Not when Hestar got to know things
I didn't.

"Do you see older boys in the seraglio?" she asked, very gently for her.

I shook my head. Men couldn't come in, but Hestar and Kral weren't
men yet.

"Boys grow into men and girls grow into women," my mother said,
almost dreamily, stroking her nails through my hair with whispers like
a blade against silk. "Boys can't learn the ways of men by living among
women, so they have to leave. But you, my darling firstborn daughter,
you may stay. You will learn the ways of women, which is far superior."

"But I want to learn about elephants." I sounded whiny, and I flinched,
waiting for the reprimand. She only laughed, smoky as the coils around
the low ceiling.

"No you don't. Those are foolish distractions, meant to keep the boys
occupied. I'll let you in on a secret, child. Men are shallow creatures,
incapable of subtlety. They are full of fire, exploding everywhere, without
calculation. You already have a tutor: me. And I will teach you far more
useful things than the names of animals you will never see."

Never see. But I wanted to. I wanted to see an elephant with a yearning
unlike any I'd ever felt. "Can I have an elephant for a pet?"

"No, that's not possible. Don't be a ninny."

That shocked me into silence.

"You are becoming a woman, Jenna—soon you'll celebrate your seventh
year. It's time for you to set aside childish things. You will be an empress
someday, if you learn well."

Just as Hestar and I had planned. "Hestar said he will be emperor and
I can be empress."

She laughed, a mocking sound in it. "What Jilliya hopes for Hestar
has nothing to do with what you can become. Do you understand? Make
sure you answer honestly. This is your opportunity to demonstrate your
intelligence. Are you as smart as I believe you to be—clever enough to
be Empress of all Dasnaria?"

Ooh, I wanted to be empress. But was I smart? *Answer honestly.* "I
don't know how smart I have to be to do that. I feel like I don't understand
anything."

With a chuckle low in her throat, she stroked my arm and pulled me against her. "That's a remarkably good answer. Of course you don't understand anything. You've been a child, living in a child's innocent world. Now you can go through your own set of doors and learn more. Do you want that?"

This time I didn't hesitate. "Oh, yes, please!"

"Your eagerness does you credit, Daughter. You remind me of myself and I shouldn't have to tell you what a high compliment that is."

Pride filled me. Hestar might have Ser Whatever, but I would have lessons with Her Imperial Majesty. "Thank you, Mother."

"But you must lose this habit of blurting out your thoughts. Immediately. Everything I teach you must be our secret. You mustn't tell any of this to anyone. Not to your nurse. Not to Hestar. No one." Her nails bit into my arm, sharp as lizard's teeth. "If you do, your hair will fall out in clumps and you'll puke up everything you eat until you die. Do you understand?"

"Yes," I whispered. I'd seen that happen to a woman in the seraglio. She'd wasted to nothing, even her whimpers fading away.

"Make your vow to me."

I took a breath. "I promise never to share what you teach me with anyone, on pain of death."

She let go of my arm and stroked my hair again. "Good girl."

"Will Inga have lessons, too—and Helva?" Though I wasn't sure if I wanted them to, or not.

"No." She breathed the word in scorn, finding a tangle and slicing at it. "Daughters learn from their own mothers. That's the way of things."

But with Jilliya so sick, when would she teach Helva? And Inga...well, Saira was kind, but nothing like my mother.

"This is your first lesson. I will tell you a story of our family," my mother said, leaving my hair alone and settling me against her, opos smoke coiling from her pipe. "Our family were the original rulers of Dasnaria. Though it was smaller then, the kingdom of Dasnaria was the richest, most prosperous and most beautiful land in all the world. Other kingdoms pledged fealty to us, envying our wealth and all that it bought. As our vassals, they thrived. And Dasnaria went from kingdom to empire. Your great-great grandfather was Emperor of Dasnaria. You are an empress by right of your ancestors on both sides. More so because our family are the true imperial line of Dasnaria."

I tried to be still as possible, like Inga's baby rabbit when the puppies came around. I'd never heard any of this, and even without my mother's warning and my own vow, I wouldn't have said any of this to Hestar. Our father, the emperor, ruled by divine right and the will of Sól, the one god.

"Jenna—look at me."

I obediently met my mother's fierce gaze.

"You understand now why you must never breathe any word of these lessons. It would mean not only your agonizing death, but mine as well."

I nodded and she stared at me a moment longer before bending to kiss my forehead, something she hadn't done in ages.

"You have the true Elskadyr fire," she said. "Everything I've done, all I've sacrificed, has been for you, so you will return our family to glory. Understand?"

"Yes, Mother," I answered, not at all honestly this time, but a creeping sensation in my tummy warned that I shouldn't say otherwise.

"The Elskadyr family will regain our rightful place and banish the upstart Konyngrrs." She sounded dreamy again, the smoke coiling thick around me. It made my eyelids heavy, but I widened my eyes, certain there would be a price to pay if I missed anything.

"When I was a girl I was gowned in the best of silks and wore pearls in my hair every day. I bathed in goat's milk and never walked in the sun, so my skin would be pure and fair. No other maid in all of the empire could match my beauty."

"What does the sun look like?" I asked, when she trailed off.

"It's beyond the doors, in the outside—a harsh and burning light in the sky. Much brighter than the chandeliers in here. It turns your skin dark and ages you beyond your years." She touched my cheek. "You needn't worry about it. Your skin is even paler than mine, even more perfect, because you live here, where the light doesn't burn. All of this is to protect you, to preserve your beauty. For you will be a great beauty. Perhaps more so than even your mother."

Her eyes glinted with that lizard coldness, making me wonder if that would be a good thing.

"You are the most beautiful woman in all of Dasnaria," I told her, "and the most highly ranked."

She smiled at me. "It was ever so. And though my father could have defeated Emperor Fritjof and taken the throne back by force, he was far more clever than that. He laid his plans carefully, my father."

"Grandfather," I whispered.

"Both of them," she agreed. "My father, King Gøren, is your grandfather and so was Emperor Fritjof, before he passed on, leaving the empire to your father, His Imperial Majesty Emperor Einarr. I was but fourteen when we wed. My father brought me to the coronation and I dazzled your father with my beauty, and my dances."

I'd heard this part before. How my mother danced for my father and he could do nothing but invite her to his bed, making her first wife. "I became the most highly ranked woman in the empire, all because I obeyed my mother and father. I am Empress of Dasnaria, reclaiming our family's birthright, and now you will continue our campaign. You will do as I did."

"I'll learn to dance like you?" I offered it tentatively, as she'd lapsed into silence again.

She laughed and patted my head. "I forget what it was like to be so innocent. So without guile. Was I ever so?"

She wasn't asking me this time, so I didn't answer.

"I doubt it," she mused. "Dancing, yes. You already dance well, and you will continue to train. One day you will perform the ducerse for the emperor and your betrothed, and all will look upon you with desire and envy. But you must practice diligently. And you must learn to preserve your beauty. Going about with wet hair is not something a future empress does. Most of all, you must be obedient. Trust that we will teach you what you need to know."

That meant no elephants, I could tell. No going out the doors.

"What about Kral?" I asked. "He's an Elskadyr, too."

"Good," my mother said. "You're thinking now. Yes, he is, but remember what I said about boys going to men?"

"Boys can't learn the ways of men by living among women, so they have to leave," I recited.

"Excellent. You will do well by memorizing what I tell you, just so. Memorize, then hold the information in the silence of your heart. This tutor Hestar and Kral go to, he is Konyngrr's man. Your father uses him to groom his sons to his own ways. I cannot change that. He will do the same with his other sons; all will belong to their father, to the world of men. Saira and Jilliya think to play this game, but they cannot. They will lose their sons and their daughters have not the mettle.

"Not like you—you are special. You are my secret weapon. Your father can claim my son, but he can't take you away from me, which means we have years to plan our strategy. The boys will have their roles, but they will have no choice but to fall into our plan. At the end you will have the satisfaction of seeing Hestar ground beneath your jeweled foot, and you'll see your brother Kral triumph. Won't that be a fine day?"

"Hestar is my brother, too," I said, realizing as I did that I sounded stubborn, not obedient. "He's my friend." And I liked him better than Kral, who could be a brat.

"I see I've left this too long. Who knew you'd grow up so fast? Hestar is your half-brother and never your friend. He already got you in trouble, didn't he? He told you things he should not have. And now you must be punished for it."

The fear returned, with sudden swift intensity. I had forgotten during the long story. Or thought my mother wasn't so angry. Seeing her now, though, I knew she hadn't forgotten. "I'm sorry, Mother," I said, meaning it with all my heart. Why, oh why had I mentioned the elephants to Kaia?

"I know you believe you're sorry." She slid her nails through my hair. "But you must be sorry to the core of your being. You must regret spilling secrets so much that you'll never even imagine doing so again. You'll learn this as you get older: loyalty enforced by pain is the only kind to rely on. Now stand up."

I did, quickly. Happy to put distance between us. My mother pulled a cord, making a bell ring, and one of her servants appeared immediately. "Send Hede."

"Yes, Your Imperial Majesty." The maid scurried off, wincing the same as Kaia had.

I stood frozen. I knew Hede, of course, as I knew everyone in the seraglio. But she never bothered us children. Still, we knew the stories, heard the servants and rekjabrel weep over their punishments at her hand. She carried a whip coiled at her waist, ever ready to deal incentive to lazy girls and recalcitrant concubines.

"Afraid?" my mother asked, her gaze sharp on my face.

"No, Mother," I said, though I didn't know why I lied that time. Some animal instinct in me unwilling to let her see that much.

She smiled, thinly, sharp lizard's teeth showing. "Because you don't yet know fear. You have no idea what it means. That, my daughter, is the next lesson. Ah, Hede. You may approach."

My mother was wrong. I did know fear at that moment. It made my legs go watery. In my head, I heard Kaia's screams for mercy. The cloying scent of Mother's opos smoke made me want to gag.

"Light whipping," the empress was instructing Hede. "No scarring, but make sure it hurts. It's time for my daughter to learn something of pain. The lesson must be memorable, but I doubt it will take much to get her attention, indulged as she's been."

If Hede answered, I don't recall. I'm not even sure what she used on me. I remember resolving not to run and then trying to escape anyway. Something impossible for my little girl self, though I fought enough that Hede bound my wrists, tying them to a ring on the wall. As my mother predicted, it didn't take much to reduce me to a spineless puddle of weeping.

The pain has faded in my memory. I mostly remember the terrifying surprise of it, the way it gutted me. And the humiliation burns bright, urine and worse running down my thrashing legs. Being naked and Hede's expressionless face as she paused, then began anew when my mother declared it not quite enough.

And Mother, watching. Asking me if I understood, then nodding at Hede to continue because each time I sobbed that I did, I did understand, that I'd never tell any secrets ever again, she said she needed to be absolutely sure of me.

I have no idea what finally satisfied her. Most likely Her Imperial Majesty watched me for signs that she'd broken me down enough. I've learned since that such techniques are developed as a refined art, and the practitioners pride themselves on knowing such things.

Afterward, she called in Kaia to clean me up. And she gave me a vial and told me to drink, just a tiny amount she said, to drive the final lesson home. With nothing in me to even question, I drank it.

And then I vomited for two days, my hair coming out in clumps, Kaia soothing me as best she could.

That part is the fever dream.

When I could eat again, Mother came to see me. I lay in bed, propped against pillows, swathed in the same numbing salve they'd given me for the lizard bite. My stomach had stopped roiling and I felt both light and hollow. Floating in nothingness.

"Show her," Mother said to her servant girl. Obediently, she held up a hand mirror. The girl in it looked nothing like me. Huge blue eyes in a face with no color but for purple shadows in the dark corners. Wisps of pale hair clung to a scalp reddened and scabbed from my scratching at it when Kaia wasn't there to stop me. Nothing left of me.

Mother sent her servant and Kaia away. Closed the door. She'd come in the middle of the day and so was dressed for court. In shining silver, draped with diamonds and pearls, her hair wound in elaborate coils, she looked like a painting.

"Your hair will grow back," Mother said. "Take utmost care of it as it does, for it will be fragile. The same for your skin and nails. Cherish your beauty, for now you understand how easily it can be taken from you. You drank the tiniest dose of poison and I can have you given more at any time. If I suspect at all that you mean to betray our secrets, I'll do it. I'd rather mourn a dead daughter than suffer your treachery. Do you understand?"

She'd kept asking me that, over and over, and I now knew only one correct answer to it. "Yes, Your Imperial Majesty."

"Do you understand why I was forced to teach you this lesson?"

Some spark in me wanted to shout at her, to fling her cruelty in her face, but I only nodded. "Yes, Your Imperial Majesty."

"Explain it to me, in your own words."

I wouldn't cry. Not ever again. "So I would know the price for disobedience and for betraying our secrets."

She smiled, ever so slightly, sliding the jeweled wedding bracelets around on her wrists. "A taste of the price. The true price would be a hundred, a thousand times what you suffered. But, because you did pay a terrible price, I shall reward you. Would you like that?"

I would, but I couldn't trust it. She came over and sat on my bed, a sparkling jewel of a woman, and caressed my cheek with her sharp nails. "It's all right, Jenna, my love, my darling daughter. The pain is behind you now. Your reward is that you will never suffer this again. Be obedient and I shall give you luxuries you cannot imagine. You will become the most powerful woman in the world. Right now, you are so powerless I could call Hede to beat you to death and no one would stop her. I can have your food poisoned and you'll die by morning. You understand that now."

My mouth dry with terror, I nodded, and Mother's smile warmed.

"You won't always be powerless. Do as I say and you will have everything. All the power. The entire world at your feet and no one able to hurt you ever again. Do you want that?"

"Yes, Your Imperial Majesty." And I did understand, deep in my hollow belly, exactly what that meant. Power was everything.

"Tell me," she murmured, a playful smile on her painted mouth. "I want to hear the words."

"I want power." My voice came out fervent.

"Will you do what you're told and set aside everything to have it? Kill for it? Will you laugh as you grind Hestar under your heel?"

"Yes." I gazed into my mother's beautiful eyes, seeing myself in them. Perhaps she would be the one I'd kill someday. And perhaps I'd laugh.

I don't know if she saw it in me, but her smile straightened and she dipped her chin, a nod of confidence and approval. "Good girl. Once you're better, we'll commence your lessons in earnest."

After she left, Kaia returned. Without a word, she changed the bedding I'd wet when my bladder voided. And when she gave me soup, I drank every drop.

Days later, when I emerged from my apartments, to the extravagant welcome of all the ladies who extolled my return to good health, Hestar and Kral had gone.

I wouldn't see either of them again for many years.

~ 3 ~

"It's not fair," Helva complained, her voice gently modulated, but her lower lip thrust out in a way that wasn't lovely at all. "Inga's only seventeen, so I don't see why she gets to go to the debut ball and I don't."

"Because it's out the doors," Inga replied, her hair a mid-process chaos of teased strands and dangling ribbons as her girls worked on it, "and you're only fifteen."

"I'll be sixteen in less than a year," she muttered.

"Which is still not eighteen, or even seventeen," Inga countered. "You're too young."

And she was Jilliya's daughter. My mother would never stomach the second wife's daughter and Hestar's full sister at my debut. Inga's mother, Saira, posed less threat. Of her babies so far, only Inga, Ban, and Mykal had survived, and Ban wasn't quite right in the head, so the gossip reported. And Inga was fourth-born to a third wife. She'd make a good alliance for the empire, but she would never be in a position to vie for the throne.

Though Helva was sixth-born, Hestar being named heir to our father had elevated her rank in subtle ways. The balance of power in the seraglio tipped almost imperceptibly with the breath of such intangible weights, despite Jilliya's inability to help her. Saira, for all her good natured smiles and gentle ways, had managed to stay strong and healthy, despite my mother's best efforts. Besides, the other ladies liked her. Normally that sort of goodwill didn't count for much, not in the face of the empress's ruthless use of her own power. But Saira had used her influence to make sure Inga would also debut that night. Something that annoyed my mother no end.

Jilliya was another story. She spent so much time pregnant, recovering from pregnancy, or miscarrying that she had no energy to conspire. Still, the emperor favored Hestar, and thus Helva, like a hand-me-down klút from Hulda herself, all the more valuable for its previous owner, rather than used. The weight of our father's favor and delight in Hestar seeped into the warmth of the seraglio like the chill draft that sometimes gusted through the doorway when someone went in or out.

Saira had plans for Inga and my mother hadn't been able to suss out what they might be. I'd tried, too, but I thought Inga didn't know. She hadn't had my lesson in keeping secrets. That lesson had been burned into my very soul. My mother had tried to enforce the custom that such a young and impressionable girl should remain behind the doors until her eighteenth birthday—or longer, if she remained not yet engaged. Saira had protested, naturally, bending the emperor's ear when she visited his bed. We knew this because he'd told my mother as much during her own bedding.

Men speak easily after sex, she'd instructed me, and have their guard down after being well-pleasured. No matter how many concubines or rekjabrel the emperor might take, a wife is superior, and knows what her husband likes. Her body might be aged, but she has the benefit of experience and noble blood. Give him exactly what he craves and then, when he's soft and sated, whisper in his ear. Saira had played on his ego to plead for Inga to be allowed to attend formal functions with the ladies who did such things. Jilliya had tried to do the same for Helva, but she could not beat my mother in ruthless guile. It hadn't taken much to put the worry that Helva, in her impressionable innocence, could be corrupted with ease, and to such an extent that it could stain Hestar's future rule.

My mother had turned it around with Inga, arranging things so my half-sister would accompany me as my attendant—and Saira not at all. A small reminder of who held the keys to the doors. Metaphorically, of course. Hede and her seconds kept the actual keys to the internal doors—and Hede obeyed only the first wife—while the guards outside kept those locks.

As for me, I had breathed a prayer of profound relief that Inga would be with me—a sentiment I'd made sure to hide from my mother. If she'd discerned that I leaned on Inga's support in any way, the empress would have seen Inga sickened or incapacitated in some way, if only to teach me to rely on no one but myself.

"But we're the only three imperial princesses," Helva continued to argue. This was another reason she fell easily to manipulation by the soft breezes of female power—Jilliya couldn't teach her the way Saira taught Inga.

Inga observed a great deal, her eyes often intent on me in a way that made me aware of the sharp mind behind them. They were a startling shade of aqua, those eyes, like our lagoon at the shallow points, where the water took on the same color as the tiles that lined it.

My own eyes were the same as my mother's, a vivid deep blue that the ladies all exclaimed over and I secretly loathed. Every time I saw my face in a reflection, I saw Hulda, Empress of Dasnaria and poisoner of my very existence.

"You look so beautiful, Jenna. Your hair is nearly the same color as the pearls, the same as your skin, and now your eyes look bluer than the deep lagoon." Helva sounded so wistful that I gave her my warmest smile. She didn't smile back. "I hate that I have brown eyes. What's brown? Nothing good!"

"Jilliya has brown eyes," Inga reminded her. "And your mother is beautiful—lovely enough to marry the Emperor of Dasnaria. And lots of good things are brown."

"Poop, and that's it," Helva declared, making the other ladies giggle.

Inga and I exchanged a glance. This was the final reason Helva couldn't attend my debut ball. She remained childish enough not to govern her mouth. Unfathomable to me, but then she hadn't had the harsh lessons I'd had on watching my words.

"Lots of things outside are brown," Inga clarified. "Like the trees of the forest."

"But have you *seen* them?" Helva demanded, her rebellious nature showing.

"You know I haven't," Inga replied with remarkable patience. "However, you and I will both see the forest someday when we leave the seraglio to marry, and I imagine it will look exactly as has been described."

"But how am I going to marry *anyone* if I never leave the seraglio?" she demanded on a much too loud wail. "I don't even know what a man looks like!"

"Enough of that," Inga snapped before I could. Our attendants had gone skittishly silent, eyes cast down, while Inga and I surreptitiously checked that none of our mothers—particularly mine—had overheard those indiscreet remarks. "You'll marry the man the emperor arranges for you," Inga continued, in a hissed voice, "as well you know and you'd be wise to not speak otherwise."

Helva twisted her unbound dark blonde hair into a knot, eyeing our elaborate braids. Kaia sat by, supervising, as my maids worked ropes of pearls into my hair, braiding as they went. Since my mother had broken Kaia's fingers as a punishment a couple of years earlier, she no longer trusted herself to tend to my hair. Her fingers had healed but remained stiff, and the joints stood out stark under her skin as she wrapped them around her ever-present mug of hot soothing gryth tea. She only drank about a quarter of what she brewed, mostly holding it to warm her hands. A good thing, as the numbing properties of the tea might ease the joint pain, but it also muddied her thoughts and made her far too susceptible to scheming by the other servants. My mother viewed my old nurse as a liability and wanted me to be rid of her, but I'd convinced her—through an admirable bit of dramatic pretense on my part—that Kaia remained a weak point my mother could use as leverage on me.

A pretense to cover the truth, which was that I loved Kaia and couldn't bear the thought of what might happen to her, now that I would be leaving to get married. It was the one dark spot in the shining star of my hope. All these years of perfecting myself under my mother's exacting gaze, training in the ducerse, of burying my hate, biding my time until I could be free—and, on my eighteenth birthday, I would finally go out the doors. I'd meet my future husband—and at last grasp the power I'd been promised.

"You're so lucky, Jenna." Helva returned to her wistful gazing, winding the rope of hair around her fingers. "You get to find out who your future husband is tonight."

I gave her a smile, echoing her delighted anticipation. Of course, I alone knew my mother's deepest and most sacrosanct secrets, how she'd worked my entire life to position me as bride to Rodolf, King of Arynherk

"And you'll see our brothers!" Helva added, slumping in her sulk.

Inga looked to me, startled. "Do you think they'll be there—all of them?"

I managed to school my exasperation with Inga. This was the result of Saira's less than accomplished tutoring. "Obviously Hestar will be there, as the heir," I pointed out. "He is ever at our father's side."

She nodded uncertainly, though I didn't see how she couldn't have heard that much of the gossip the rekjabrel and concubines brought back with them. I should teach her, it occurred to me with sudden and brutal reality. Tonight the emperor would reveal my future husband—though, if all had gone according to my mother's scheming, with the considerable assistance from the Elskadyrs, the candidate would come as no surprise to us, at least—and within a few days I'd be married. After a week of newlywed bedding, I'd be gone, which meant Inga and Helva would be on their own against my mother, who would no longer have the project of molding me.

I should have thought of it before, what my final birthday and marriage would mean, but actually leaving the seraglio remained a concept I almost couldn't wrap my mind around. Helva had a point, that we'd heard the outside world described—but the vastness of things like forests, mountains, and oceans you couldn't see across, remained nearly impossible to imagine. I'd study the palm trees planted in artful clusters around the tiled lagoons, and tried to multiply them into thousands, and the image would stutter and fail entirely.

"Palm tree trunks are brown," I said, the thought occurring to me, "and dates. Those are sweet."

Helva scowled at me. "Not the same color at all."

"That's because your eyes are such a deep brown," I told her, feeling generous in my chagrin that I hadn't considered what my sisters would face in my absence. Her scowl didn't fade, so I abandoned that effort. "Her Imperial Majesty told me that all of our brothers will attend," I told Inga. Though it hardly counted as privileged information, my stomach tensed at the reveal, and I found myself scanning for my mother, though I knew she was already at court. She had been all day, receiving the many visitors who'd traveled to the Imperial Palace for my debut. "Hestar will be my escort and Kral will be yours."

Inga clasped her hands. "Why didn't you tell me? This is wonderful news!"

Helva promptly burst into tears, her nurse hastening over to comfort her. "Hestar should be *my* escort," she hiccuped between sobs. "Or I'd take Leo and Loke, or baby Harlan. Even Ban!"

"Perhaps Her Highness should rest," Kaia suggested to Helva's nurse, with a pointed look at the pot of gryth.

Helva didn't even resist as her nurse urged her to drink the soothing tea, and she went off obediently enough to her early bed. They'd no doubt ply her with enough to keep her sleeping until morning. Hopefully by then she'd be in a better frame of mind and we could tell her stories over breakfast about the ball and give her news of our brothers.

With Helva gone, Inga and I fell into companionable silence, the quiet of sisters who understood we couldn't really discuss everything we wished to, not with so many eager ears around us. Besides, the thing we most wished to discuss—who I would marry—remained a mystery, at least to her. We'd already spent the last several years speculating what my husband would be like, with me pretending total ignorance. Which wasn't far from the case. Though my mother had schooled me in womanly arts—maintaining beauty, ferreting out secrets, the complexity of human nature and how to manipulate it—she'd never shown me a portrait of Rodolf, or told me much about him.

It wouldn't do, after all, for me to slip and let it be known that I knew more than a woman should. She'd equipped me with all the tools I needed to assemble the knowledge of the empire into the framework she'd given me. Everything would fall into place once I left the seraglio as wife to a powerful king. For the King of Arynherk was the most powerful king—that's why the empress and my Elskadyr family had picked him—it only remained to be seen if the emperor had chosen as they had plotted he would.

Tonight I would meet my father, the emperor. I would see my childhood playmate, Hestar, along with my one full brother and four other half-brothers, Even baby Harlan, the last boy to leave the seraglio—at least of our immediate family—whose sweet nature I'd missed more than I'd imagined I would. And I would meet my Elskadyr grandfather. The moment loomed ahead of me.

In a short time, my world would explode.

I'd go through the doors, and at last begin to fully live. Inga caught my eye, her smile slight and appropriately restrained, but her extraordinary eyes glittering bright with excitement. With Helva gone, we could show our delight.

With our hair finished, our ladies began the intricate task of wrapping us in our fancy klúts, the finest we'd ever worn—ones for grown women, not girlish ones for lounging about the seraglio. Inga's was of turquoise silk, a shade deeper than her eyes, and the delicate silk shimmered with hints of violet and green as it snugged around her waist and emphasized her generous bosom. She wore little jewelry, as befitted an unmarried maiden, but the simple silver chains adorning her throat and wrists shone with elegance. Her finger and toenails had been polished a subtle silver, too, and her ladies draped her klút to frame her slender bare feet, the silver rings on her toes connected to the graceful chains that looped to her ankle bracelets, all studded with aquamarines.

A woman's feet reveal her status, and ours were perfect in every way.

I wore more jewelry, as a betrothed woman. Mother had given me the Elskadyr pearls she'd worn to her wedding. They suited my virginal status, and would also serve to remind my future husband—and all present—of the wealth of the Elskadyr family.

"And you, the greatest pearl of them all," Mother had said the night before when she gifted me with the heavy chest. Kaia had to call three girls to carry it back to my apartments. "You will shine like the jewel you are, until your husband can think of nothing but having you for his own—the most valuable of all his treasures."

"But... I will be first wife, yes?" I'd asked, pausing in my gleeful enjoyment of sliding a rope of pearls as long as I stood tall through my fingers.

The empress gave me an impatient look. "You are His Imperial Majesty's firstborn daughter—of course you'll be first wife."

I breathed an internal sigh of relief. The phrasing that put me as one of his treasures had given me a start. I would not wish for a life such as Saira or Jilliya led. I'd been obedient all this time so I would have the power my mother wielded.

More, even.

And so I wore white. Pearlescent white, the shimmering silk matched to my skin over painstaking weeks of effort, the dye girls suffering under my mother's whip-sharp attention and Hede's actual whip. Other ladies had spent the entire morning gluing opalescent shells to my finger and toenails, extending them to elegant lengths and filing them to perfectly matched and even rounds. I'd been wearing practice ones on my toes for months, so I'd learn to walk and dance without breaking them off.

With the priceless silk so fragile, so carefully perfected with effort and suffering, I had not worn it until this moment. Where the quantities of pearls weighed on me like nothing I'd felt before—from the swaying bands on my feet to the strings of them wound into the hair falling down my back—the klút seemed to be hardly there at all. Perhaps because it matched my skin so exactly, it seemed as if all of me showed through.

Surely not, though, for that would be unforgivably immodest in an imperial princess. Still…

"Do I look all right?" I whispered to Inga.

Her face showed guileless sympathy and she took my hand. "You look like a pearl come to life. You will dazzle them all."

"You will," I returned, wishing I could be the one wearing the lovely turquoise klút.

She shook her head. "No one will notice me. I'm happy to be in your shadow. I'm so excited to go with you!"

I squeezed her hand. "This will be a night we'll remember always, and we'll tell our own daughters the story."

"Always," she agreed.

~ 4 ~

Side by side, though no longer hand in hand, as it would ruin the lines of our klúts, Inga and I walked to the great doors of the seraglio.

They were very old—as old as the Imperial Palace itself, my mother said, as the seraglio had been built first—heavy and ornate. Hede herself guarded them, her dark eyes surveying us, an odd smile on her hard mouth. "All grown up, our imperial princesses," she said, her eyes lingering on me. Ever since the night she'd stripped and beaten me at my mother's bidding, Hede's gaze felt unclean to me, as if she forever saw me that way, helpless and weeping under her lash.

I met her eyes boldly, keeping my chin at an imperious tilt. I would leave this place and she'd live out her days here as my mother's puppet. She would no longer have power over me. That felt good, too.

As if receiving that message, Hede bowed to us, unlocked the doors, and opened them. She banged on the opposing doors. Where the ones facing the seraglio were ornately decorated, inlaid with jewels and tiles that matched the rest of our home, the outside doors were featureless. With no locks or keyholes, they sealed close together, made of heavy iron, black and dull with it. As kids, we'd sometimes tried to hide nearby, to catch a glimpse of those other doors when some of the ladies went out or returned, but there wasn't much of a place to hide.

That made this my first time to see them up close—and their dour ugliness disappointed me. Hopefully that wasn't an omen for all of the outside world, though Mother always emphasized the magical perfection of the seraglio compared to the outside.

Hede banged on the doors and a small slot opened in one, at eye height. It closed as fast as it had opened, then the massive door—only on that side—swung wide. More women stood outside. Not gray-garbed servants with their shorn heads, and not rekjabrel, concubines, or noble ladies, but women like Hede. They had hard eyes and carried whips at their belts. Belts made of leather, like their garments. I'd seen leather, but only in small pieces, usually holding beads for stringing onto more graceful wires.

They gestured us forward, and I led the way, as we had to go single-file through the narrow opening. A long stairway rose above us, rising nine steps to a landing, then turning to rise again. Relieved that our mothers had made us practice this, too, albeit on the much shorter flights of stairs that led to some of the ladies' apartments, including my own, I laid a hand on the rail and began to ascend, carefully setting my feet to preserve the long toenails. Inga did likewise on the other side. We'd both been scolded repeatedly to resist the urge to gather our klúts in our hands. The meticulous draping meant we didn't need to, but the habit remained. The silk we wore, however, would show every stain from an inappropriately sweaty palm.

Imperial princesses did not sweat.

Indeed, it seemed unlikely I would, as chill air filled the stairwell. I shivered, my nipples going tight with it, and I fervently hoped they wouldn't show through the barely-there silk. Fortunately, the light remained dim, not even illuminating the shadows. My feet sank into the plush carpet of each step as we climbed at a serenely slow pace. Though my heart fluttered with exhilarated excitement, I focused on slow breathing, controlling it as I did while dancing. Beside me, Inga did the same. We must appear as unruffled as a still lagoon, providing a perfect reflection to the world.

Our guards followed several steps behind. Courteous, but oddly they did not make me feel safe as I'd expected.

We reached the top, and one of the guards stepped around us to unlock the doors. They handed us over to another pair of lady guards just like them, complete with identical whips. All this time, Inga and I had not spoken and we still didn't. But she caught my eye and raised a perfectly arched brow just a twitch. I had to look away not to laugh, grateful again to have her with me on this long walk.

For it was longer than I'd ever walked before. I'd thought the seraglio large, but the palace that surrounded it stretched on forever. Of course, I'd understood that the seraglio lay in the heart of the Imperial Palace, nested within it like a child protected in the womb. But I'd somehow pictured it as just slightly bigger—enough so we wouldn't rattle around. Now I understood that my home, the small seraglio, was like a single pearl within a great, bulky chest.

Which made me much smaller than that. Though an imperial princess doesn't sweat, a cold line of it formed under the weight of my pearl-laden hair, dripping down my spine. I felt impossibly tiny and vulnerable. Ironic how much I'd looked forward to leaving the seraglio—and now all I wanted was to run back to its warm safety and the security of the enclosed space.

"When does it end?" Inga whispered, and in her face I glimpsed the same terror that sucked at me. No longer caring if it disturbed the pristine lines of my klút, I took her hand, and she clutched mine gratefully.

"Seven more doors, Your Imperial Highness," said one of the women behind us, an older one with gray hair in a bun. "Just count and you'll be fine."

It was a kindness she offered us, a rare one that evening. The counting did help as we followed one corridor lined with closed doors on either side to another set of locked doors at the end. Our guards would bang on them, the sound of locks would echo through the metal or wood, and the doors would swing open, allowing us out again. Then, at the fourth set of doors, we saw our first men in the flesh.

We'd been braced for the encounter. The other ladies had warned us that seeing men for the first time would be alarming. They'd shown us paintings of them, to help educate us. Those images, however, did little to prepare me for the reality.

They were *big*. The two men, garbed in imperial blue, the Konyngrr fist embroidered over their hearts, towered over us, their shoulders twice as wide as ours, with hands as big as my face. These didn't have facial hair as some of the paintings had shown, but their faces looked hard and foreign anyway. They wore swords and knives—also things I'd only seen in paintings—though I couldn't imagine why they'd need such things, as huge and strong as they looked. Even Hede would be no match for men.

And the way they looked at me... my skin crawled as if a spider had escaped from a date palm and skittered under my klút. Inga cringed against me, her hand slick in mine, and I remembered to avert my eyes. A good reason for that rule, as looking men in the face clearly led only to this sapping fear and sensation of being naked while clothed.

"Their Imperial Highnesses Princesses Jenna and Inga," the bun woman snapped, her voice like metal. "Make your obeisance."

From the edges of my vision, I could see the men bow deeply. "Lucky us, to draw the shift where we get to be the first to lay eyes on the imperial princesses," one of the men said, his voice low and growly like a dog grown too big for the seraglio.

"Greetings, Your Imperial Highnesses," said the other, more smoothly, but with a voice just as low, so it resonated deeper in my bones than in my ears. "Forgive us. Your loveliness has rattled our feeble brains. You honor us with your beauty."

Bun woman hmphed and gestured us past them. We went, faster than we had, but I still remembered, even in my relief, to be careful of my toenails and the delicate strands of pearls decorating my feet. Behind us, the men laughed, a coarse sound that made me want to hunch my shoulders. I felt sure they laughed at some joke about us.

"Don't mind them, Your Imperial Highnesses," bun woman said. "All of this is for your protection. They would never harm you in any way."

And yet, I felt that they already had, on some invisible level where an intangible bruise already purpled. Looking back on this, I understand how deliberately we were manipulated. We could have been gradually introduced to the world outside the seraglio, to the presence and ways of men. Instead, over the course of a few hours, Inga and I were barraged with the new and—by its very nature—terrifying world outside. Like newborn kittens, we stumbled out, wide-eyed and seeking approval, and they set the dogs on us.

It left us with no ability but to be obedient, as that provided the only safety left to us.

The same pair of guards stayed with us until the final set of doors. Both women bowed to us and bun woman wished us well—I don't even remember her exact words, everything had become a dull roar in my ears.

As numb as if I'd drunk a pot of gryth tea, I stepped through the final doors and onto a balcony rimmed by a fanciful railing. Directly before us hung a chandelier easily three times my height, made entirely of crystal and lit by thousands of candles. This wasn't the soft, warming light of the seraglio, but one like the weapons the men wore, sharp and shattering.

Below the rail, a dizzying drop to a grand room larger than the seraglio, and filled with more people than I'd ever seen in my entire life. They sent up a roar, making me want to stick my fingers in my ears. When Inga tugged our hands apart, I thought that must be why, but she dropped her hands to her sides. "Appearances!" she hissed at me.

I couldn't imagine how she could be thinking of such things, but she had it right. We had one responsibility tonight: to be serenely beautiful. The crowd of people continued to cheer and I pasted a smile on my face, wondering if the cold sweat popping out all over my skin showed to them. The mob quieted and two men ascended the curving stairs to either side of the balcony.

Big, as all men were. Tall and blond, with swords and carrying flowers. The one on my side wore mostly silver, blindingly bright. Inga's was in deep blue, but with far more silver than the guards. Mine stepped up to me, a tentative smile on his face.

"Jenna?" He said my name like a question, then proffered the elaborate bouquet of white flowers. "It's good to see you again."

I searched his face, seeing nothing of my childhood playmate. "Hestar?"

He nodded. "Who else. I brought you something."

He held out a gray thing, and I took it awkwardly, balancing the bouquet in one arm while trying to keep the flowers from touching the delicate silk of my klút. An animal, but not alive. A toy. Still remarkably lifelike. My memory stirred.

"An elephant," he said, somewhat impatient. "Don't you remember?"

I did, and it made me feel ill to recall that day. That endless night, and the long recovery that followed. Though he likely didn't know any of that had happened to me. "Thank you," I said, reaching for my best poise, which seemed to have abandoned me somewhere around the second set of doors. "It's a lovely gift and I shall treasure it."

He nodded again, seeming pleased. Then offered an arm. I knew I was to take it so he could escort me down the curving staircase, but with the flowers in one arm and the elephant in the other hand, I didn't know what to do. I hadn't practiced this part.

"Here." Hestar took the elephant from me and tossed it to one of the guards at the door. "You can get it later."

I took his arm, glancing over to see that Inga had done the same with the other man, who must be Kral. Leaner and more handsome than Hestar, with sharp cheekbones and icy blue eyes, he touched a finger to his temple.

"Hello Jenna." He grinned at me, seeming much happier to see me than Hestar had. Though my mother had warned me, hadn't she? Kral was my full brother and blood looked after blood. "You've grown into an incredibly beautiful woman." He glanced down at Inga and patted her hand where it rested on his forearm. "You both have."

"Indeed," Hestar agreed.

"The four of us, together again," Kral declared, still smiling widely. "Everyone is so excited to meet you. Ready?"

We agreed that we were. Despite all we'd gone through already, however, we had no idea just how not ready we were.

~ 5 ~

It all reminded me of being poisoned. The incessant noise, the too-bright light, the oppressive heat of so many bodies pressed around me. People spoke to me and I couldn't process what they said. I clung to Hestar's arm, kept my gaze modestly lowered and murmured the polite replies my mother had drilled into me.

Later, they told me I had presented the perfect image of virginal innocence and maidenly propriety. Exactly what they'd molded me to be.

I lost sight of Inga, though occasionally her turquoise klút caught my eye in a vivid flash. The men I could hardly tell apart. I couldn't have picked out Kral from the other men given all the time in the world, much less the bare seconds afforded me before someone else introduced himself.

And they were almost all men, and almost all looked me up and down, speculating and making me feel that skin-crawling naked vulnerability. After exchanging greetings with me, along with the standard phrases praising my beauty, they inevitably began speaking only to Hestar. They deferred to him, as obsequious as the lowest tier rekjabrel kowtowing to a wife. For his part, Hestar puffed and strutted. Things outside weren't so different from the seraglio after all, however, and I began to discern who Hestar thought worthy of his time and who he couldn't be bothered with.

It reminded me starkly of our one afternoon of playing emperor and empress. Except he'd continued to play the game and I'd fallen out of practice.

So far, I felt no more powerful than before. And somewhere, in the still back corner of my mind, the part of myself that managed to remain calm and undazzled by the array of sensory input, I began to suspect a cheat.

Occasionally the men were accompanied by women—an event that came as both a relief and stirred my curiosity. They took me in with equal interest. The Prince of Robsyn spoke with Hestar at length while the woman on his arm gave me a friendly smile. She wore an elaborate gown of foreign style, with a high neck and long sleeves, and a hugely full skirt that trailed on the carpet, hiding her feet.

Amazingly, she wore her dark blonde hair cut off at the shoulders, though it fell in pretty curls and seemed purposely styled that way. With her noble manner and rich garb, she clearly wasn't a servant, and she didn't avert her gaze at all, but studied me with frank appraisal similar to a man's, only without the unpleasant feeling that came from it.

"It's all a great deal to take in, I imagine, Your Imperial Highness," she said in a low voice, the way I might speak to Inga and Helva when I hoped our attendants might not overhear.

"Yes." The affirmation escaped me in a gush, and I had to restrain myself from reaching out to embrace her. "It is…" With horror I realized I had no idea who she was. I had not learned women's names in my studies.

"Princessa Adaladja, of Robsyn," she provided. "A fairly distant and minor kingdom in your vast empire." She leaned in, lowering her voice further to a conspiratorial whisper. "And of little account, no matter what my Fredrick might hope." She slid her husband a fond smile.

"Ah," I replied, faintly and like a ninny. I had no idea how to receive such information. My mother would see it as a sign of weakness. Or was it an attempt to fool me into underestimating her so she could blindside me? The politics of the seraglio hadn't prepared me for this… barrage of information.

"Your outfit is gorgeous," she told me, the warmth in her eyes making me believe she meant it sincerely, "but aren't you cold?"

"Cold?" I echoed. Yes, my feet were freezing and it seemed like I hadn't felt warm since I left the seraglio. But I wasn't sure if I should admit to that. Surely not.

"This is my first visit to the Imperial Palace," Princessa Adaladja confided. "Such a to-do passing all the guards to enter this fortress! And I'm sure I've never been so cold in my life. I've spent the entire two days since I arrived bundled under furs as close to the fire as I could get without singeing myself." She laughed heartily and I smiled uncertainly, her amusement infectious.

"Then you should visit the seraglio," I invited. "It's very warm in there."

Her eyes brightened with interest. "Can I? I didn't know if anyone not a member of the Imperial Family was allowed."

Oh. I didn't know either. Though the only rule I knew of was that only females—and boys younger than seven—could enter. Still… yes, there had been visitors. My mother and Saira had entertained female guests, inviting them to lunch. Jilliya never did, but she hardly stirred out of her apartments. Surely what the wives could do, the imperial princesses could do also. Inga, Helva, and I had just never had anyone to invite before. It might soothe Helva's envy, to have a foreign visitor.

"Yes," I said, feeling a bit more powerful with the decision. "Perhaps you could join us for luncheon tomorrow?"

"I would *love* that! I confess I've been insanely curious about the seraglio. Don't you mind, not seeing the outside world?"

"One cannot miss what one has never had," I told her.

She sobered, cocking her head. "I'm not sure I believe that."

I regarded her with some astonishment. Not believe? A person didn't simply decide not to believe in the truth.

Princessa Adaladja glanced at her husband, still deep in conversation with Hestar, both ignoring us utterly. "I had a bird once," the princessa said, "when I was a girl. A gift. It had been hatched from the pet bird of one of my mother's friends and I'd admired it so. All white—really an ivory very like your own hair, Your Imperial Highness—with long wings and a tail that trailed like a lady's train." She sighed at the memory. "And so clever. I taught mine to say words."

"Words?" I gasped, laughing, and her eyes sparkled in shared delight.

"I swear to Sól! She knew her name—Clio—and she could ask for cookies, dates, and she could call my cat so convincingly that Isabel would come running as if I'd called her."

"How miraculous," I breathed.

"Yes. I loved her so." She saddened, shaking her head. "But she forever gazed out my windows at the sky. And sometimes I'd hear her whistling at the birds outside, imitating their calls."

I knew what windows were, for some of the apartments in the seraglio had them, overlooking the lagoons and so forth. But the concept of windows opening to the outside arrested me. "Birds fly around outside?" I asked. "How are they recaptured?"

The princessa blinked at me. "They aren't. Most birds live wild, not as pets."

Wild. I knew the word, but had never heard it used that way. *Wild.* Not undisciplined and in need of punishment, but free. Not a pet.

"That's the point of my story," Princessa Adaladja continued, "though it's gone longer than I intended and I'm realizing I've perhaps misjudged in telling it to Your Imperial Highness."

"No, finish it," I commanded. She regarded me oddly and I added, "If you please. I'd love to hear the ending."

"All right." She glanced at her husband again. They seemed to be finishing. Hestar was scanning the room beyond him, which she also noted, so she hurried. "One day, I couldn't stand it anymore, her sad little whistles. So I opened the door to her cage. It was a warm summer day and the glazing was off the windows. At first she didn't move. Just looked."

"Maybe she was afraid." My heart trembled at the words.

The princessa smiled at me. "Who could blame her? The cage was all she knew. I went to lessons with my tutor and when I returned, the cage was empty and Clio was gone."

"Did she ever come back?"

Princessa Adaladja shook her head, her smile a blend of happiness and regret. "No. Not exactly. I saw her from time to time. In the trees or flying overhead. My mother was very angry with me for losing such an expensive gift, but I didn't care."

This princessa astonished me at every turn. "Even when she punished you?"

Princessa Adaladja stopped smiling. "Punish me? Why, no. I—"

"I believe we've monopolized Their Imperial Highnesses long enough, my sweet," Prince Frederick interrupted, offering Adaladja his arm. "Delightful to meet you at last, Your Imperial Highness Princess Jenna."

I received their bows and murmured polite replies.

"You seemed to get on well with the princessa," Hestar observed.

"Yes." I peeked at him from the corner of my eye. "It was a pleasure to make acquaintance with another woman."

Hestar laughed, not at all nicely. Not like Adaladja's joyful one. "I'd think you'd have had your fill of women by now."

I didn't reply. As to that, I felt I'd already had my fill of men.

* * * *

After more of the same, for so long that my feet had begun to throb, a gong silenced the gathering. Hestar's arm tightened, then relaxed. Deliberate, in my estimation. He beamed down at me, this smile quite fake. "Ready to meet our father, His Imperial Majesty?"

It sounded like a taunt, and for the first time I truly believed this was the boy I'd known. My playmate had taunted me exactly thus, pushing me to climb higher and run faster. "And my future husband," I reminded him.

Hestar grunted, a man sound I had no context to interpret. So I said nothing more, simply allowed myself to be led into the throne room. The crowd parted for us, creating an aisle for our stately procession. Hestar at least knew to adjust his booted steps to my mincing ones. Kral and Inga fell in behind us and she gave me an encouraging smile. But her lovely eyes looked glassy and her fair face paler even than the false sun the seraglio gave us. She was as overwhelmed as I, making me wonder if it showed so clearly on me. I looked ahead, raising my chin even as I kept my eyes from meeting anyone else's, even the other women's. Easier and safer that way.

I was an Imperial Princess, firstborn daughter of the Emperor of Dasnaria, and I would not shame him.

At the grand doors, a servant took my bouquet and I unbent that arm with gratitude—and some stiff pain, it had stayed crooked so long. Because we entered first, the vast hall echoed empty. At the fore, an immense throne towered over the room. Suddenly I understood the words of that long ago rekjabrel. Made of mirror-bright platinum, the throne shone with light so blinding I could hardly look upon it. Crystals and diamonds studded the surface—more of the former than the latter, to my practiced eye, as at least I knew jewelry well—and refracted the light of the elaborate chandelier suspended above it.

But Hestar and I had gotten it wrong in imagining the throne like any other chair. I should have guessed that it would be shaped like that Konyngrr fist, though open. His Imperial Majesty sat in the palm of it, the fingers stretched out to curl around him. The web of the Dasnarian Empire radiated out from behind him, represented by sparkling wires, also encrusted with crystals. Each thread ran to a sculpture set in a niche on the towering walls, embodying the primary product of that kingdom or province. Bjarg's granite. An apple tree for Eikrik. I knew about those places, but couldn't imagine where in the outside they might be. But easier to look on those than the dazzlingly painful brightness of the throne and the emperor himself. Even if I were allowed to gaze upon him directly.

From what I could see through my peripheral vision, my father sat high up, his feet well above my head. Framed by a velvet cloak in a blue so deep as to be almost black, then armored in polished platinum, the emperor wore a modified helm as his crown, inset with the Imperial Diamonds.

My mother stood at the foot of the throne, a familiar sight in her deep blue klút, studded with more of the Elskadyr pearls. Oddly, I felt happy to see her. Such was the toll of the evening, of adjusting to everything outside the seraglio, that I should be pleased and grateful for my mother's presence. Princessa Adaladja's story hung with me, her voice whispering images into my mind of a world even more immense than this. For all that the size of the Imperial Palace, the mob of people crowding it, and the grating feel of men's eyes on my skin discomfited me to the point of panic, this was but a single building within the even larger outside.

How could I have ever wanted this?

The cage was all she knew.

And I knew myself to be frightened of leaving mine.

Inga had drawn up beside me, Kral on her other side. I studied her bare toes, still so pretty in their silver jewelry, but tinged blue with chill like mine. I'd have the servants heat water for us to soak our feet when we returned—that would be a lovely treat. And we could wrap up in heavy silk throws like the elderly ladies used and we could discuss all we had heard and seen. It would make more sense then.

Looking forward to that, imagining telling her about the princessa's talking bird, I studied our toes and waited as the people assembled behind us. The room finally fell silent.

"My daughters." The voice boomed over the room, echoing off the marble walls and making the crystal studded wires whisper with sound. "We welcome you to court at last, flowers of the Dasnarian Empire, my greatest treasures. Princess Jenna, step forward and raise your face to me. Allow your father to look upon you."

I might have stayed frozen to the spot if Hestar had not dropped my arm and stepped back with a bow. I made myself move forward and, steeling my eyes not to flinch from the brightness, raised my face as ordered.

Within the helm, my father's face showed—one very like Hestar's, not so much like Kral's, who looked far more like our mother. And like me, I realized. Us, with our high Elskadyr cheekbones and slender builds. Our father was broadly built, and Hestar had his wide shoulders. Both of them had our father's eyes, however, icy as blue diamonds, very nearly colorless, and totally lacking all warmth. I shivered as my father surveyed me. By a flicker in his expression, he noted that weakness, I felt sure.

"You may lower your eyes, Daughter."

Feeling the reprieve, I did so.

"A pearl beyond price, indeed," he mused. "Even more beautiful than you were at her age, isn't that so, Hulda mine?"

"Your Imperial Majesty flatters me," my mother replied in the softest voice I'd ever heard her use. She sounded very nearly as submissive as the lowest rekjabrel. "Though I might note that, by the time I'd reached Princess Jenna's age, I'd already borne you two children, such was my imperial husband's mighty virility."

He chuckled. "Soon we shall have grandchildren, I predict, if this daughter of yours has inherited your fecundity along with your beauty. What say you, Daughter—are you prepared to meet your husband?"

I'd practiced for this. I knew the words. My throat, however, had gone tight and cold. I couldn't even swallow, much less speak.

"His Imperial Majesty asked you a question, Princess," my mother said, and I knew that tone well. Hede might not be nearby with her whip at the ready, but she would be waiting for me when I returned to the seraglio. I had not yet escaped, not yet grasped the power that would open the door to this particular cage. Time to speak up.

"If it pleases you, Your Imperial Majesty," I said, surprised to hear my voice as smooth and melodious as my mother could ever wish it to be. "I am ready and grateful to receive the attention of the husband Your Imperial Majesty has chosen for me."

"Well spoken," the emperor said, sounding pleased indeed, and his approval warmed me. "She is more shy than you ever were, Hulda. Far more becoming of an Imperial Princess. You've done well. Now, let me see my other grown daughter. Princess Inga, raise your face that I may see you."

I waited, watching Inga from the corner of my eye as she also endured inspection. She did better than I, looking enviably calm and lovely. When our father commented on her remarkable eyes, she blushed prettily and thanked him for noticing. She spoke the flowery words with such grace and ease that a stab of envy pricked me, that Inga should have pleased our father more than I had. But he'd approved of me, hadn't he?

He had. I could be generous and allow Inga her moment to shine in his gaze also.

Still … Saira must have rehearsed it with her. She hadn't been able to conspire to be present herself tonight, but she could influence Inga—and through her, the emperor, Hestar, Kral…and even me. It made me realize the ways in which Saira had reached out from the seraglio regardless.

And it made me reconsider Inga's friendship. I'd been so glad to have her with me, but obviously Inga hadn't come along simply to hold my hand. As her conversation continued with our father—he clearly charmed by her pretty phrases—I breathed to stay relaxed and not betray my ire with something as easy to observe as a clenched jaw.

In the edge of my vision, my mother shifted, ever so slightly, but catching my eye. Seething with fury, she flicked at a pearl on her klút, clearly communicating that I was currently failing the Elskadyr family and I'd better take control of the situation. But how?

Though I supposed I hadn't been dismissed. I hadn't stepped back—Inga had stepped up level with me. Dare I interrupt? They spoke cozily of all the dances Inga could perform. Ones I also knew.

"My sister dances that one beautifully, Your Imperial Majesty," I slipped the remark into a moment when Inga paused to consider her words. "When she is my age, she will no doubt be my equal in her skill, perhaps even the ducerse someday."

In the corner of my eye, Inga allowed her lips to settle over whatever she'd been about to say. She lowered her eyes and slid me a look from the side.

"Aha!" The emperor pounded a fist mailed in mirror-bright, intricately worked metal on the arm of his throne, which happened to be the upturned thumb. "She is your daughter then, Hulda. I'd begun to wonder, with her so meek. I remember you dancing the ducerse when you were also so young and nubile. Does our daughter exceed your skill in that as she does in beauty?"

I didn't dare peek at my mother. I didn't need to. My emotional umbilical cord still stretched between us, feeding me her rage and jealousy. Even as I quailed internally, imagining what her revenge might be, sympathy also stirred in me. Though the empress deserved pity less than any woman in the seraglio—the opposite, as her iron rule of everyone generated more sorrow than joy—I couldn't help but wonder at her life. I'd never imagined our father would treat her with such casual cruelty. From the smile I glimpsed on his face, via a quick look as he focused his attention on my mother, I could see he enjoyed it, too.

How horrible to be married to a man who mocked your age. Yet I knew he found my mother desirable still. He brought her to his bed every few days, even with the empire sending him the most beautiful concubines and rekjabrel for his pleasure. My mother knew him inside and out, so she'd often told me.

But for the first time, I doubted.

I knew my mother lied, easily and without qualm. She'd taught me to do the same, for a woman's lies are her weapons as much as poison and knowledge of the sensual delights. For some reason, it had never occurred to me that she might lie to me also.

"Perhaps Your Imperial Majesty will be the judge of that," my mother was saying, her voice without flaw, revealing none of how she felt. "Tomorrow evening, at the betrothal feast, Jenna will dance the ducerse for us all. It's time the imperial court bear witness to your pearl beyond price."

"An excellent idea." The emperor sounded jovial, though the exchange had been only a formality, as my dance had been long planned. "And it's well known that a husband's affection shall be cemented by his desire. What say you—will you see your betrothed dance the ducerse, Rodolf?"

Rodolf. The name sang through me with a thrill of triumph. My mother had done it. Wealthy. Valiant. A warrior to the core. Ambitious. His kingdom of Arynherk held preeminence over all within the empire, as the largest and richest—and also the most recently acquired by Emperor Einarr. And his lands bordered the Elskadyr homeland, Pyrna. With me as queen of Arynherk, we could combine forces with Elskadyr and overthrow the emperor. Hestar would never sit the throne; my son would.

So excited I almost couldn't keep my modest posture, I nearly popped my eyes out of their sockets, straining to catch the first glimpse of my husband without overtly scanning.

A movement to the side of the throne, and a man stepped forward. King Rodolf's representative? No. The man himself, with that iron crown upon his bald head. A thin strip of gray hair bordered the bottom of it, merging into a long beard that covered his copious jowls. He wore matte dark armor over broad shoulders, so I couldn't see his body, but his face was lined with age, eyes burning coal-dark in deep sockets surrounded by sagging tissue.

Fixed on me, his lust crawling over me, puffy lips damp with it. "Oh yes, Your Imperial Majesty," he replied in a voice accustomed to shouting. "The only thing that could please me more is our wedding night, when young Jenna will dance for my private pleasure."

~ 6 ~

Despite my earlier uncharitable thoughts, I fervently wished for a moment with Inga. She always had a way of seeing the good in things, rarely allowing disappointment to slow her stride. Rodolf might not be that bad. I'd simply built up an image in my head of what my husband would be like. A silly girl weaving fantasies from painted images—and those of other men, not even him.

Of course he wouldn't be young. For the power and influence we needed, my husband would have to be a man of mature years.

But I hadn't expected *old*.

"Your Imperial Highness Princess Jenna." Rodolf bowed before me. Court had adjourned, the attendees streaming out to the ballroom. Hestar remained at my side, but Kral had led Inga off.

"Your Highness King Rodolf," I murmured, desperately grateful I didn't have to look him in the eye. His boots looked handsome and fine, though the steel tips on them gave me pause. What purpose did they serve? Not only for decoration, as they were not shiny, but dark. And sharp.

"You are everything I could have wished for and more," he informed me. His voice throbbed with repressed excitement. "His Imperial Majesty favors me greatly with such a pearl and I shall treasure you for all the days of your life."

All as I'd dreamed my betrothed would say to me on our meeting. And yet, all wrong. I didn't want these words from him. With a bolt of terror that made my bladder want to void, I realized I didn't want to marry this man.

And I had no choice.

"Thank you, Your Highness," I managed to say. The captive bird, knowing a few words to speak.

"Now, now—we're to be husband and wife. No sense with long titles between us. You may call me 'sir.'"

"Yes... sir." It didn't seem right that I, an imperial princess, should address a lesser king as 'sir,' but he was to be my husband, which made me subject to him in all things. Mother had said I was to obey him. Something that had sounded much easier when I'd imagined him as something... other than this.

"A paragon, you are. I have a gift for you."

Though I'd been prepared for this, too, I flinched when he took my hand. Far from being angry, however, Rodolf smiled. "So sensitive," he murmured, for my ears alone. "I relish that in you, my bride." Holding my right hand in a firm grasp, he slid a ring onto my middle finger. The Arynherk diamond. Long, with pointed ends like blades, it fit perfectly. I'd been measured for it, after all. "The Arynherk diamonds go well with Elskadyr pearls, don't you think?" He admired the ring on my hand, turning it this way and that. "Your wedding bracelets will be equally lovely on you. I can't wait to see them."

I murmured a vague assent. Plenty to appease him.

"Come my pretty thing," he said, offering me his arm, "let us go observe the dancing. If His Imperial Highness Prince Hestar allows?"

"I'm to keep her in sight at all times," Hestar agreed in good cheer, "but I doubt even you, Rodolf, could divest lovely Jenna of her virginity in view of all the court."

Rodolf laughed, phlegm in it. "Her beauty begs a man to attempt it." He patted my hand, then pinched the skin of my forearm hard enough to make me gasp. "But I can wait two nights for this prize."

They fell into talking as we walked, exchanging hunting stories, of all things, ones that quickly turned gruesome. I concentrated on walking, as Rodolf strode much too quickly. One of my long toenails snagged on the carpet, snapping off, and I stumbled slightly.

"What's this?" Rodolf demanded. "Clumsy girl."

"I apologize, sir."

"That's all right, my sweetmeat." He caressed my arm again in that way that made me want to snatch away and run. "You're young yet and will learn. Once you're safely ensconced in my seraglio, you'll never have to walk again. I'll have you carried to my bed on the richest of litters!"

I eked out a smile. Enough to satisfy him. My mother's training at work. She'd taught me how to smile through the cruelest of insults, and now I understood why.

All too well.

* * * *

The evening dragged on. Endless and grinding. I'd long since passed the point of overload and feeling any emotion at all. I felt simply exhausted. Inga, two chairs down from me, looked no better. Rodolf and Kral sat between us, preventing any conversation, and Hestar sat on my other side, conversing over my head with them both. I watched the dancing, not even enjoying the sight, much as I'd longed to see it, to hear music played on instruments, rather than chanted by women's throats.

Mostly the men danced, bold displays of strength and athleticism, shouting each other on to greater feats, urging the musicians to play faster until some men dropped off the dance, hands raised in surrender, others collapsing on the floor in laughter. Occasionally, a dance would call for male and female partners—a much smaller crowd, with so few women present, and even fewer allowed to participate. Which meant I spotted Princessa Adaladja easily. Her full skirts flared as she spun in the dance and she danced the complicated steps with enthusiastic speed, clapping with perfect tempo, and laughing up at her husband.

Though still far older than I, Prince Frederick would have been far easier to stomach than my own betrothed. Envy made me feel ill, that Adaladja should have so much—a handsome husband, talking birds, windows to the outside, dances!—when I, firstborn daughter to the first wife of the emperor himself should have none of that.

The diamond weighed heavy on my hand and I longed to throw it across the room.

"Mother wants you to know you're performing beautifully," Kral said, leaning over the chair Rodolf had vacated. He and Hestar had gone off on some quest to have another man settle some argument between them, leaving Kral to chaperone both Inga and me. As the pair of them had grown increasingly loud and belligerent with mjed, I'd breathed a sigh of relief at their departure.

Now I glanced at Kral from the corner of my eye. He nodded at me. Beyond him, Inga spoke with another prince, her voice so soft I couldn't make out what she said.

"You're doing the Elskadyr family great honor," Kral said meaningfully, raising his brows over icy blue eyes. He'd be Inga's age, just as Hestar was mine—but somehow they both seemed so much older and harder. The way of men and women, I supposed, for them to be like the swords they carried and we the silk-swathed sheaths they rested in.

"How fare you, sister?" Kral asked, a slight line between his brows. "You seem tired."

"I am tired," I confessed. "And thirsty." I also needed desperately to empty my bladder, but I had no idea how to convey that need to my brother. Would I have to travel all the way to the seraglio and back?

Kral raised his brows in surprise, as if noticing my empty hands for the first time. "Why have you no refreshments?"

"Mjed is not appropriate for a woman," I pointed out.

He laughed, sounding exasperated. "There are other beverages. Hestar is an ass," he added, in a lowered voice. "Come with me. No need for you to sit here with Rodolf off arguing who bagged the biggest buck in last autumn's hunt. Inga, would you like something to drink?"

Inga glanced over sideways, relief evident on her face. "Sól bless you, I would."

Kral raised his eyes, as if looking to Sól. "Save me from meek females who won't ask for what they need." He stood, crooking out both elbows for us, escorting us off the dais. He, too, seemed to know to measure his stride. Happily, for I'd been hard-pressed enough to hide my broken toenail under a fold of my klút. I could hardly hide another.

"Sisters, dear." Kral spoke quietly. "Would you perhaps also like a moment of privacy to adjust the folds of your klúts?"

I glanced down at my klút in puzzlement, then noted the direction of his subtly pointed finger—a door through which several rekjabrel emerged. "Oh yes, please. Thank you, brother!" I averred.

Inga frowned. "Your klút looks lovely, Jenna, I don't—"

I raised my brows at her. "Privacy," I emphasized. "To attend to womanly... appearances."

Understanding dawned. "Oh... Oh! More blessings on you Kral."

He grinned, pleased to have pleased us. "One moment." He stopped one of the rekjabrel. "Check that it's all clear within for the imperial princesses."

She bowed deeply and scurried to comply, returning immediately and holding the curtains open for us, bent nearly in half in her obeisance. "Your Imperial Highnesses."

"I'll wait for you here." Kral said, and turned his back to the door, arms folded, clearly intending to stand guard. We hastened in, as best we could and still maintain a stately glide.

"I thought I was going to burst," Inga whispered.

"Me, too." And we both giggled, sighing in relief. "I thought we'd have to walk all the way back to the seraglio," I confessed.

"Same. And I doubted I could make it. I imagined myself as a wee one, piddling on the carpet of one of those long hallways."

We finished, washing our hands side by side in basins of warm water with floating lemon slices, just as in the seraglio.

"Jenna," Inga said quietly, hesitation in her voice. "How are you—"

"Not here. Later." If I'd learned nothing else from my mother, I knew that even an apparently empty room could hold listening ears. "How does my klút look?"

"Perfectly folded." She met my eyes, sympathy softening hers. I hated her a little for it.

"Now we know how to ask," I said briskly, moving past her.

She touched my arm, where a bruise formed already, then picked up my hand with the ring. "It's very beautiful," she said.

"Yes. A great honor to marry such a wealthy king. Come—our brother promised us refreshments."

She followed after, saying nothing more.

* * * *

The honeyed juice Kral found for us soothed and refreshed my throat. He also settled us into a semi-private corner with a small grouping of low couches and pillows, surrounded by curtains on three sides.

"The rest of our brothers are looking forward to saying hello, if you ladies are willing," Kral said.

"Then they *are* here." Inga brightened.

Kral rolled his eyes at us. "Where else would they be? Except for Ban, of course," he noted. "He's off training with the infantry."

Of course. Kral seemed to have no concept how little we knew. "We hadn't seen them yet, is all," I explained, though I hadn't been sure of it. None of these men looked like the little brothers I recalled.

"I'll wait for one of them to circle by, then get him to send for the others. We hoped that as the evening wore on, we'd have this opportunity to talk amongst ourselves, since we can't come to you. Leo, Loke, and Mykal are all nearby, keeping an eye on this nook."

"And Harlan?" Inga asked.

Kral made a face. "Who knows where that rabbit has got to. Cowering with the other bunnies, I imagine, baby that he is."

"Barely younger than the twins," I reminded him, finding that rhythm again. Once Kral had been the boy I forced to wait on me, tasking him to get Leo and Loke to wheedle treats and jewels out of the other ladies.

Kral grinned, maybe remembering, too. "But they are all only half-brothers to you, whereas I'm your full brother, thus far superior."

"Oh gracious." Inga waved her hands at us. "We're not reunited two hours and already we're squabbling over who is half and full? We're all children of His Imperial Majesty."

"True, true," Kral agreed amiably, but slid me a look that communicated the opposite. "Loke! There you are. Get the others." He glanced at Inga. "Harlan, too," he added, somewhat grudgingly. "And bring some mjed."

Within moments, two identical young men with bronze hair stepped in and bowed. When they straightened, they both grinned at us. "Sisters!" the one holding a flask of mjed exclaimed.

"You look just the same, only prettier," said the other.

"You don't," I told them. "You've grown up so."

"I bet I still know which is which, however," Inga said, sounding mischievous.

"Guess then," said the one without the mjed.

"I don't have to guess," I inserted. "You are Leo."

"And you are Loke," Inga agreed.

They both looked surprised. "Most people can't tell us apart."

"We're your sisters," I informed them, exchanging looks with Inga. "We always could." We shared a secret smile. We'd never divulge our long-ago system for identifying which was which, no matter how they'd tried to fool us.

Two other younger men arrived. One looked enough like the boy he'd been to make me feel a little less bewildered. Harlan trailed behind the older young man who must be Mykal by a few steps, carrying two tall glasses of juice, both of them stopping to bow to us. Mykal looked like a younger version of Kral, with the same icy blue eyes, though a bit of softness kept him from having the same shark leanness. Harlan had the broader build of our father and Hestar, already taller than Mykal and the twins. Like Helva, he took after Jilliya in his expression, a gentleness to his gray eyes. "Helva isn't here then?" he asked.

Kral cuffed him on the side of the head. "You were at the assembly. You know she's not. And what are you—a handmaiden to fetch and carry refreshments?"

Harlan, who hadn't spilled a drop of the juice despite the blow, handed the glasses to us and rubbed his ear. "I thought she might be able to come later," he explained. "A reunion of sorts, for all of us. I haven't seen her in seven years."

"She's too young," Kral dismissed. "We're lucky they let Inga out." He grinned wickedly. "Now tell us all the gossip of the seraglio. The rekjabrel have naked girl-on-girl orgies in the little lagoon, don't they? Tell us the truth."

Mykal blushed bright red, goggling at us. "They do? I don't remember that."

"Of course they don't!" I admonished Kral, but Inga had dissolved into giggles.

"Do you remember," she said to Kral, "how we used to sneak about and spy on the little lagoon, hoping to catch the rekjabrel kissing each other?"

He laughed and sat beside her. "Of course! We made that hiding spot and put old palm fronds on it so they couldn't see us."

They fell into conversation, reminiscing over the old games, and I felt a pang that Hestar hadn't come along to do the same with me. No one needed to tell me, however, that we wouldn't be having this cozy little family party with Hestar present. He'd grown and changed beyond all of us, harder and with his gaze firmly focused on the throne. I wouldn't mind so much, depriving him of it, having spent time again in his presence.

Still, some part of me mourned my childhood friend.

"So," Loke said, "in two days you'll marry Bloody Rodolf."

Leo elbowed him hard. "Don't call him that."

The four of them sat in a ring around me, leaving Kral and Inga to their conversation.

Loke looked blank. "Why not? You call him that. We all do."

"Because he'll be Jenna's husband," Harlan inserted, sounded grave beyond his years. "You'll frighten her."

I nearly laughed at that, as if they could frighten me more than being actually married to the man would. "Why do you call him Bloody?" I asked. Mother had said he was a fierce warrior—hard to believe, seeing him tonight, but clearly he'd aged.

They exchanged glances, Loke clearly realizing his error. "No reason," he muttered.

"Tell me," I commanded in my best big-sister voice. "I might as well know what I'm getting into."

None of them would meet my eye. Finally Mykal, scratching his head, still red-faced, said, "You're his fifth wife. Or will be, rather."

"Fifth?" Indignation rose in me. Also a surge of hope. I could break the engagement on those grounds. I'd been promised first wife and nothing less. "I was told I'll be his first wife."

"Oh, you will be." Loke actually snickered, then flinched when Leo elbowed him harder, punching him in the shoulder.

"Cut it out," Harlan ordered and they subsided, though Loke sneered at him. Harlan didn't notice, his calm gray eyes on me. He leaned forward, elbows on his knees. "Jenna—his other wives are all dead."

Dead? I gaped at him before I remembered myself, sipping the juice to cover my shock. "All…four of them?"

"One after the other," Loke explained with gruesome relish.

"All in their twenties," Leo added.

"Suspiciously," Loke finished, unnecessarily.

Had I felt ill before? My head swam, though fear seemed a distant concept. All of this had been too much.

"We thought you should know," Harlan maintained, his gaze steady.

"It won't happen to Jenna," Mykal announced with staunch pride. "She's an imperial princess, and Bloody Rodolf needs an heir. He's desperate. Everyone says so."

Leo and Loke shushed him. Kral glanced up, frowned, but replied to something Inga said, returning his attention to her.

"You have your family," Harlan told me, and the other three nodded with enthusiasm. All of them so earnest in their youth.

I wanted to laugh and weep, both. Hestar had to know about Rodolf. My mother and father both knew, too. I had my family and that same family would wed me to this man whose wives had all perished. The ladies of the seraglio might be insulated from much of the outside world, but we were not deaf and dumb, not fools. The wives and higher ranked concubines lived better lives than most, but even they suffered occasionally from an outburst of lust.

And the rekjabrel… well, they suffered more than occasionally. The lucky ones went on to be servant girls. The others we never saw again.

~ 7 ~

By the time Inga and I limped back to the seraglio, we parted ways for our own apartments with barely a murmured goodnight, we were so worn out. Foot-soaking and gossiping would have to wait for morning. And then we both slept so long—the quiet of our dim rooms viciously guarded by our nurses—that Helva had worked herself into another frenzy by the time we met, yawning and heavy eyed, for a late breakfast.

"Finally!" Helva yipped like one of Jilliya's little dogs. "Tell me everything. Start at the beginning. *Everything.*"

She looked far too rested and bright-eyed. And had groomed herself to perfection. Helva's hair rippled in bronze waves—very like Leo and Loke, I saw now—and she wore a violet klút that brought out the gold flecks in her dark eyes. Compensating, most likely, for missing out on being fitted out like we had been the night before. She certainly outshone us this morning. Like me, Inga wore an old robe, not flattering, but cozy and soft. Neither of us had yet bathed and we both still wore the dregs of makeup from the evening. Kaia had nattered at me, but I'd managed to keep upright only long enough to be divested of all those cursed pearls. I refused to sit still for bathing. By the look of her, Inga had felt the same.

Rodolf's diamond, of course, had not come off and never would again. It weighed on my hand like an iron manacle.

"Tea, then gossip," Inga declared, earning my eternal gratitude. I wrapped my hands around my own delicate cup and gulped it down, blistering my throat and glad for the burn. I wasn't completely numb. The servant girl refilled it and I drank that one more slowly, aware that Helva had her gaze firmly fixed on the diamond ring, eyes soft with admiration and envy.

"Your ring is so beautiful, Jenna," she crooned, fingers twitching to touch. "Can I see it? When you're ready of course," she added, flicking a glance at Inga who'd leveled a stern look on her.

Tempted to fling it at Helva and tell her to keep it for all I cared, I held out my hand across the small table, still cradling my tea in the other. For years the three of us had sat at this triangular table by the little lagoon for breakfast. Crafted of white porcelain and inlaid with flowers made of precious ivory in subtle shades, a guild of craftsmen had sent it in tribute to us, the three imperial princesses. We loved it and it remained ours alone, the place we lingered over our tea, nibbled cakes, and dreamed of how our husbands would be. I'd never once imagined I'd feel this way the morning after my betrothal. Wretched. Terrified. Trapped.

It was probably better we hadn't talked the night before. Without the time to sleep on things, to mull them over as I lay drowsing and half-asleep that morning, I might have said the wrong things. As it was, I still didn't have the right words—only a bit more caution about saying the wrong ones.

Helva cooed over the spectacular diamond, turning it so it caught the soft light from above, sending sparkles of multi-colored fragments, shattering across the porcelain table. We had chandeliers, too, I realized. A version of those in the grand halls of the outer palace, but ours were turned inward. Rather than tiered confections of brilliant crystal, the ones in the seraglio shone light from curved and frosted lenses, emanating warmth and glow. No one ever lit candles in them and, for yet another first time, I wondered where the light came from.

"It's gorgeous. Unbelievable. You could buy a kingdom with this gem alone, I bet," Helva was saying, her hand gripping mine like a constricting snake intent on keeping its prey. "Just think of who's worn this before you, all the grand queens and empresses!"

And at least four dead women. I found the strength to pull my hand from hers. Inga observed that with a raised brow. "King Rodolf may not be all we dreamed of for you," she said, very softly and soothingly, "but a mature man can bring many fine qualities to a marriage. He might make a kind and generous husband. And you'll have children to love. You'll live in Arynherk, see more of the world."

Helva had started shimmying in impatience for Inga to finish her speech. I felt much the same, but for different reasons. Inga had been having her happy reunion with Kral. She didn't know what our other brothers had told me.

"King Rodolf!" Helva burst out, clapping her hands together. "Fantastic! Oh, congratulations, Jenna. Well done!"

Inga set a cautioning hand on Helva's arm, but said nothing, a line between her golden brows. Not understanding, as Inga clearly had no more words either, Helva shook her off.

"What? Why aren't you two over the moon? He's the one you wanted! The top of the list. Everyone knew it."

True. Even Hulda's considerable skills of intimidation and intrigue hadn't kept the speculation quiet. For easily a year, practically since the day after my seventeenth birthday, the favorite topic within the seraglio—and without, as the servants and rekjabrel brought back gossip from the rest of the Imperial Palace—had been who the emperor would favor with my hand in marriage. Even sequestered as we were, every woman and child in the seraglio understood that the imperial princesses would serve to consolidate His Imperial Majesty's hold on the empire. Who we married would speak loudly and clearly of our father's favor.

And yet my mother had never once mentioned his age, his inherent cruelty. That his many wives all died young.

That I wouldn't be gaining power, but losing it utterly and completely.

"What does he look like?" Helva wanted to know, still blissfully oblivious to the undercurrents. "Is he like King Niklas in the tapestry? Stalwart and daring! Does he have dark hair like that—then maybe your babies won't be all boring blond. Or red! That would be lovely, too. Why aren't you saying anything? Jenna!"

"His hair is gray," I snapped, "what there is of it. I have no idea what it was when he was young."

Unkind of me, perhaps, but at least Helva began to catch on. And it stopped her inane babble. "Gray? Then he's... older. But just mature. Mother got her first gray hair just after her thirtieth birthday—remember? She actually screamed. Her maids thought she'd hurt herself and—"

"Helva," Inga broke in, far more gently than I could. In fact, I set down my tea cup, wary of shattering it in my hands. The servant girl refilled it, but I only stared into its depths. As if it would hold any answers for me. "King Rodolf is mostly bald because he's *much* older. I imagine he's of an age with Old Mara."

Helva blanched, horrified eyes going to mine for confirmation before she remembered herself and smoothed her expression. Old Mara had celebrated her seventy-eighth birthday and was the oldest lady in the seraglio. She'd been our great-grandfather's favorite concubine and, following his death, left to her own devices to age gracefully and sedately in the seraglio. I'd once overheard a group of rekjabrel speculating that Mara had lived so long because she hadn't been called to serve in over fifty years. They'd said other things I hadn't understood, about how one night in the entertainment salons felt like it took years off their lives.

Anticipating such intimacies with Rodolf seemed to be aging me as I sat there. I understood what they might have meant all too well. In two days' time, I'd be sitting at this table, understanding more than I'd ever wanted to. Inga had taken over describing Rodolf for the avidly curious Helva, demonstrating judicious discretion in her choice of words. Though the servants had stepped away, they'd be listening as avidly as Helva—and the news would soon reach every ear in the seraglio.

I gazed between my sisters at the little lagoon, the still waters mirror smooth and untouched. It had been ours, also, for years, left for the exclusive use of the imperial princesses, giving us the illusion of privacy, with the draping ferns bordering it and the row of palm trees that screened the rest of the seraglio. Allowing us to pretend we lived in a garden rather than a sequestered room within a fortress of a palace. Our gilded cage.

Both of which reminded me of Princessa Adaladja and my invitation.

"Gracious!" I exclaimed, utterly chagrined, even panicked. "I forgot I invited Princessa Adaladja for lunch here."

"You did?" Inga looked beyond surprised, and Helva squealed in delight, clapping her hands.

"A guest! A real princessa!"

"You're an imperial princess," Inga reminded her.

"I know, but I've never met *another* princess. Besides you two. And she's from *outside*. I'm so excited. I should change clothes!"

"You look lovely," Inga said in a dry tone, giving me a betrayed look. "Whereas I look like I rolled out of bed. Which I did. If I may say it, so do you, Princess Jenna. When will the Princessa be here?"

"I don't know. I've never invited anyone to the seraglio before. You know that."

"I do, so I'm surprised you did. Which was she?"

"The dark-haired woman in the ruby red gown—the one that stood out all around her."

"Ah, I didn't get to meet her. So, how did you invite her?" Inga prodded. "Hulda taught you the protocol, I'm sure. Helva and I will need to know this, too."

An excellent question. She, as always, was absolutely right. We were growing up and taking our places in the empire as imperial princesses. I might be going off to another, even worse cage, but Inga and Helva would have some time yet to entertain the other noble ladies of the realm.

Still, I could simply fail to follow up. Surely an informal invitation uttered in casual conversation counted for little. And I'd carelessly offered in the glut of being overwhelmed, before I'd found out … everything else. Not carelessly. I'd been sincere, because I liked the princessa and wanted to talk with her more. Because Helva deserved a treat.

Helva who watched me with hopeful eyes and a diligently closed mouth, though she was clearly bursting to plead with me. They both read it in me, that I might decide to renege. Given my crushing emotional state, no one would blame me.

But that would be giving in. Besides, I had no intention of risking my mother's ire by expressing my true feelings about the engagement. Not where I could be overheard by anyone lurking in the ferns. I had no doubt of how she'd enforce my obedience.

So I summoned Hede.

* * * *

It turned out to be remarkably easy. I was, after all, an imperial princess. My powers might be limited to the seraglio, but within that small lagoon, I held rank arguably second only to my mother's. If I wished to, I could make things difficult even for Saira and Jilliya.

Hede simply bowed and agreed to pass the message that Princessa Adaladja should be escorted to the seraglio to meet the three imperial princesses for lunch in two hours' time. A late lunch, but we seldom stuck to any particular schedule in the seraglio anyway, with the servants always poised to deliver whatever we wanted, whenever we asked.

This time, however, I went to some trouble to order our best delicacies. The princessa might think we lived in a cage, like her sorrowful bird, but she would see we at least lacked for no luxury.

Inga had already hastened off to bathe and dress properly. Helva went off to peruse her vast collection of klúts, and perhaps have her nurse re-do her hair, though we both reiterated that she didn't need to.

Truly, I didn't blame her for being excited. Only yesterday, I might have felt the same.

Today I felt desperate for distraction. Tonight I would dance the ducerse for the court. Something I'd once looked forward to—demonstrating my hard-earned grace and proficiency—and now dreaded second only to my wedding.

And wedding night.

Don't think about it.

* * * *

We received the princessa in the luncheon salon where my mother entertained her visitors. She had tutored me in this, that the formality of the curtained dining space gave outsiders a more secure feeling of being received as they would at any palace, where they had designated rooms and tables for such events. She might not have expected me to act so soon, but I felt confident she'd approve—or at least, would not castigate me—as long as I followed the letter of her customs.

Amusingly enough, the salon we used was the one that Hestar and I had long ago commandeered to be our throne room. I'd call it ironic but the seraglio wasn't so large that we had many spaces like it. And it wasn't as if I hadn't been in that salon countless times over the ensuing years.

Perhaps seeing Hestar again the night before made those memories weigh as heavy on my mind as Rodolf's bloody diamond on my hand. How we'd played at being emperor and empress. How in my childish naivete, I'd believed we'd somehow rule together. Back then we'd been equals in the seraglio—just a little boy and a little girl, both too juvenile to be defined as anything else by the world.

Then he'd gone out the doors and become this powerfully big and important person, while I'd remained behind, the stunted twin robbed of her vitality by the stronger one. Had our positions been reversed, would I have condemned him, this sibling I hadn't seen in a decade, to such a fate? I couldn't imagine doing such a thing to Inga or Helva, certainly. Nor to any of my brothers, for that matter.

Except maybe to Hestar, in revenge or punishment. He who stood by, making jokes while Rodolf spoke of … I couldn't think about it.

Still, I thought, watching my reflection as one of my girls brushed out my hair, drying it to a shimmering gleam, if I'd been born a male, I might think differently. Turning my face from side to side, I imagined my jaw harder and wider. The high cheekbones delicately dusted with rose to accentuate the angles of my face would have that hint of gold stubble like Kral's, and be heavier, my nose less fine. Though my eyes would be the same deep blue, they'd be less fringed, the brows not plucked into elegant lines. My skin wouldn't be pearly white, but kissed by the hot sun of outside.

And I'd have no heart. I'd laugh about tracking animals that dragged themselves bleeding through the forest, their guts hanging out. I'd drink and grow loud and obnoxious with it.

I'd view women as weak, pretty things to be draped around my neck, then tossed aside when they broke.

I left my hair hanging long and loose, only a single strand of pearls threaded in to hold it off my forehead. Princessa Adaladja had met Her Imperial Highness Princess Jenna the night before. Today I wanted her to know me as Jenna, another woman.

What was I thinking—that we might be friends? Perhaps, though I knew full well that where I was going, I would have no friends. I wouldn't even have sisters. If the women of the seraglio at Arynherk were anything at all like the ones at the Imperial Palace, I'd be feared and envied, but no one would be pleased to have me there, disrupting their carefully balanced power structure.

You'll have children to love, Inga had said, ever optimistic. That could be. But if I had sons, they'd be taken from me, and if I had girls ... I'd sooner drown them than send them to the fate that awaited me. I paused as I passed the little lagoon, partly ours because it lay so close to my apartments, where Inga and Helva always came to me. Deep enough to drown myself in, if I had the courage, and planned it so no one found me in time to stop me. A rekjabrel had done that, tied her klút so it had deep pockets of material and then filled it with everything heavy she could find.

How long had she fought the urge to slip out of the klút and strike up for air before unconsciousness took that temptation away? Longer than I could, most likely. I'd never possessed much courage that way.

Mother had a knack for bleeding away unattractive defiance.

Helva, of course, was already in the dining salon, meticulously rearranging the place settings to perfect the spacing. She had changed her klút. And her hair. It must have taken most of the intervening two hours for her girls to weave the gold ribbon into her hundreds of tiny braids, twisted into a crown studded with topazes that matched her klút of shimmering bronze silk. Her face fell into tragic proportions as she caught sight of me.

"You didn't dress up!" she wailed.

"I told you not to. I had a surfeit of being so polished I couldn't move last night, and I'll have to dress in my dancer's costume tonight. I wanted to be comfortable for a while longer."

Besides, that polished and glamourized version of myself had begun to feel like a fraud. That's who they would marry to Rodolf, who I would perforce become. As long as I could, I'd be myself.

Inga arrived, her hair also loose, setting Helva into a frenzy of despair over whether she had time to take hers down, too. The sight of Hede leading the princessa around the big lagoon put a stop to that. I took Helva by the shoulders. "This is how you wanted to present yourself, so be that person. Don't question that. Be yourself. You're an imperial princess—the honor is all hers, a gift to have luncheon with you."

Helva gave me a crooked smile, relieved and delighted. She hugged me, carefully, so as not to crush the creases of her klút. "You're the best, Jenna. I don't know what we'll do when you're gone. I shall weep every day."

It hit my ears so much as if I'd already died that I had to take a moment to catch my breath again. Fortunately my mother's training took over, and I fixed a smile of welcome on my face, turning to greet Princessa Adaladja.

~ 8 ~

She wore a gown easily as gorgeous as the night before—and in much the same style—though less jewel-strewn. Curtseying deeply, she gave me a warm smile as I gave her my hands to help her rise.

"Your Imperial Highness—you look equally stunning 'at home,' if not more so." She plucked at her own gown. "I was in a dither deciding what one wears to luncheon in the seraglio at the Imperial Palace. I expect I've overdone it, just as Freddy predicted."

"Nonsense," I assured her. "It is you and my sister, Her Imperial Highness Princess Helva, who put us to shame."

Inga picked up the thread easily. "Yes, I'm afraid Jenna and I are still recovering from all the wonders we witnessed last night. You clearly possess far more resilience. We didn't formally meet last night, but I am Inga."

"And you may call me Jenna," I added. "When we are 'at home,' as you say, in the seraglio, we rarely use titles with each other."

"Then you must call me Ada," she agreed. "The other is such a mouthful. I curse my mother for it daily."

"I wasn't allowed to go, or I would have made sure to meet you," Helva burst out. "You're so lovely. How do you make your skirts stand out like that? Are you naked beneath or does it go all the way through—and if you're naked, don't you get cold drafts?"

Ada regarded Helva in frank astonishment. Inga clapped a hand over her own mouth, as if that would somehow mute Helva. And I burst into laughter. I couldn't help it—and it felt so much better than the dread that had been throttling me.

Fortunately Ada joined in, smiling easily and seeming not at all offended. Though that could have been excellent manners on her part.

"Thus the reason our little sister isn't allowed to go to balls yet," I commented drily, though I couldn't help thinking the evening could only have been improved by Helva's unstudied enthusiasm and curiosity.

"Since we are all women here," Ada replied, lifting the hem of her skirt, showing us the layers of ruffled material beneath—complete with boning to give it structure. "And, no, I'm not naked beneath that." She lifted the boning on one side to reveal a sort of feminine trousers such as the little boys wore. "However—and I hope you don't find this impertinent, Your Imperial Highness—but most ladies of my station would be most taken aback to be asked about their nakedness in any context. For future reference."

"Ohh," Helva breathed, blushing deeply. "I offer my apologies."

"None needed," Ada replied. "I have a sister your age who is also curious as a cat. And your gown and hair are so lovely, Your Imperial Highness. I love how your hair looks like a crown."

"And I love the things on your feet. So pretty! What do you call them?"

Ada paused a moment, puzzled. "My slippers?"

"Slippers," Helva repeated, rapt. "Nobody here has those."

Ada looked to me in question. "I know the women of the empire traditionally go barefoot, but you don't have shoes of any sort?"

I shook my head, disguising that I'd been studying the slippers in equal fascination. "How could we wear our foot jewelry then? Besides, Robsyn is part of the Dasnarian Empire."

"Oh, of course we are. And utterly loyal to His Imperial Majesty. I didn't mean to imply otherwise."

"We'd never think it," Inga put in gently, though not entirely honestly, to my mind. Not that I'd question Ada's loyalty for making such a remark, but my mother certainly would.

"Thank you, though I apologize, regardless, for my thoughtless words. I meant that Robsyn retains many of our long-held customs and does not share everything with parts of the empire closer to Jofarstyrr. Provincial of us, I'm sure. We only wish we had foot jewelry such as yours."

"You may have some of mine," Helva offered. "I'll show you how to wear it." She pointed her pretty foot, draped in gold chains studded with more topazes.

"You are more than generous, Your Imperial Highness." Ada curtseyed to emphasize her appreciation.

"Why isn't she calling me by my name?" Helva asked me out of the corner of her mouth. Not at all discreetly, though Ada pretended not to hear.

"Because you didn't give her express permission," I murmured back.

"Oh! Please call me Helva. And I'm naked under my klút. That's all we have. Because, you know, a klút is really all you need."

Inga closed her eyes briefly and how Ada kept a straight face, I had no idea. But she nodded in interest. "Is it all one piece of material then?"

"Yes, I can unwind it and show—"

"Perhaps not before lunch," I suggested quickly.

"Or not at all," Inga agreed. "As we don't offer to undress for our guests. I'm thinking Jilliya is remiss in your lessons, sister of mine."

"Well, my mother tries," Helva confided to Ada as we sat, "but she's tired a lot. And she says my mouth is wider than the big lagoon and my thoughts pour straight out without pausing for inspection."

"I used to have the very same problem," Ada told her. "Discretion comes with maturity, I believe."

"Oh, do you think so? That would be lovely."

We sat and the servants brought us lunch in successive courses. Ada praised each with such perfect courtesy that I wished I could prod Helva to pay attention and learn from her. I could only hope she'd absorb some of it.

"The seraglio is extraordinarily beautiful—more so than I imagined. I'm only sorry that I had such a brief glimpse as I was escorted in. While this salon is lovely, it's a pity we can't see out. Is it possible to have a tour after?" Ada inquired.

"If you like, I'd be pleased to oblige," I replied before Helva could. "And if you'd like to be able to see, that's easily accomplished." I signaled to a girl, who then scurried off. Shortly she and several others unhooked the curtains, opening the salon on three sides.

"Oh how wonderful!" Ada exclaimed. "But rather less private."

I started to raise a brow, but felt too much like my mother, ready to lay down the law of the seraglio. Fortunately Inga and Helva laughed, merrily enough not to be insulting.

"There is no privacy in the seraglio," Inga explained with a gentle smile.

But Ada didn't return it. She looked...intensely disturbed. "None? Never?"

"Assume everything you say will be overheard and you'll be fine," I assured her. "Just as at any public event."

"But when do you... Never mind," she corrected herself, resuming a happy mien, though this one deliberately applied, rather than genuine, I believed. Ada wasn't that different from us, in that I couldn't discern her façade from sincerity. All women everywhere no doubt learn those skills early. With the dramatic exception of Helva, but she would learn, too. Hopefully not via a fatal mistake.

Either way, I would not be there to witness it or help her pick up the pieces. Odd how life works—the same time the day before, I'd been bursting with the excitement to leave this place forever and harbored no such dark thoughts. It spoke to the shallowness of my nature, I supposed, that only when I dreaded what lay before me did I spare a thought for those I'd leave behind.

And it all made me feel morose, where I'd invited Ada to entertain us and take my mind off my misery.

So I focused on the princessa, absorbing her stories of Robsyn and their foreign ways. Helva asked nine questions for every one of mine or Inga's, which Ada bore genially, graciously answering every one. Had I not glimpsed the moment she donned her mask of discretion, I'd have thought she spoke with artless frankness, rather that the carefully crafted replies that omitted what must be details she considered too dangerous to be bandied about.

Still, when we'd finished, Ada turned to me. "Jenna, might I impose upon you for that promised tour? I'll let our other charming companions return to their days which they so graciously interrupted for me."

"But we don't have anything else to—" Helva began before Inga shushed her.

"A delight to meet you, Princessa." Inga inclined her head, pulling Helva to her feet. "We shall leave you to it. Enjoy your tour."

"Shall I apologize for young Helva again?" I asked with a wince, once they'd gone.

Ada laughed, rising and brushing out her skirts. I had no idea how she sat in such things without bending the insides all out of shape. "She is charming. As are you all, though you and Inga seem to have been considerably more schooled in … word choice, shall we say."

"Ah. I take your meaning. Helva's mother, Jilliya, is also His Imperial Highness Prince Hestar's mother. As heir, he's received much of her focus. And Jilliya is often indisposed. Saira, Inga's mother, will hopefully take Helva under her wing. Let us start here, at the big lagoon. As you can see, the bit bordering our dining salon is a small pool off the main one. As this is the biggest and deepest, it's popular with most everyone."

We followed the walkway to the noisier section of the lagoon, where children, nurses, and rekjabrel played games. Older ladies looked on, including Old Mara, ensconced on her favorite settee, pot of tea beside her.

"Do all the women of the Imperial Palace live in here?" Ada asked, bright eyes taking in the scene.

"They all are welcome to. Some have apartments in the between spaces, such as where you are quartered. But those are primarily concubines, some highly ranked rekjabrel, and female guards for them. Some are servants who must live with or close to those ladies, in order to be constantly available."

"I have two who live in my suite, it seems. I wondered about that, if they live there all the time."

She looked so troubled that I put a hand on her arm. "It's an honor for them—and intended as one for you—for them to be with you at all times. They would not live there by themselves when there is not a guest. We are not so cruel as to isolate any woman like that, especially outside the security of the seraglio. Not unless she was being disciplined, in which case she wouldn't be assigned to serve such an august personage, such as yourself."

Ada slid me a sideways glance. "May I ask you a personal question?"

"Of course," I replied, keeping my pace serene, ignoring the instinctive flinch. If I didn't care to reply honestly, I'd simply lie.

"Are you happy here—living in the seraglio?"

"Very happy, yes." An easy reply.

"Would you say the same if we could not be overheard?"

She'd chosen her opportunity wisely, the noise of a group of children splashing likely to cover our words. Still, I gave her a pleasant smile. "My words are the same in all places, regardless of who might listen."

Ada nodded, the unhappy turn to her mouth showing she didn't believe me. "I have a confession to make," she began.

"At this end of the big lagoon," I said as a group of scantily clad rekjabrel passed us on the way to swim, "are the apartments of Her Imperial Highness Jilliya and her retinue. She is second wife, mother to Helva and His Imperial Highness Prince Hestar." Once the group passed, I added under my breath. "Confessions are valuable currency here. Be wary of how you spend yours."

Ada took a breath. "I'd hoped to speak with you more privately. Is there truly nowhere?"

"No, I can't show you Her Imperial Highness's apartments as she's not well and mustn't be disturbed, but would you care to see mine? They are all much the same."

"I would love that!" Ada enthused, perhaps more loudly than she needed to, but the line worked. I guided her around the wide end of the big lagoon, along the path through the flowering shrubs. "How is it that these can grow indoors?" Ada trailed her hand over the lush blossom. "All of these plants should need sunlight."

I gestured to the lights above. "These give us all the light and warmth they require."

She tipped her head back to study them, a line of thought between her brows. "But false light—candles or torches—isn't the same as the sun. I can't grow a plant indoors only by lantern or torchlight."

"I don't know," I admitted. "They simply do."

"Does anyone come in to maintain, or replace them?"

I shook my head. "Servant girls who live here have the responsibility of trimming the plants, removing dead leaves and such, but they grow and flower on their own."

"There's a legend," Ada mused, "that the original core of the Imperial Palace was built by a sorcerer king, long ago. Perhaps he created the enchantment that enabled this place to exist—and to stay so warm, even at the bottom of a frozen lake."

"Frozen lake?" I echoed. "This is the little lagoon, which only Inga, Helva, and I use. It's our private place."

"Charming, too. So lovely and peaceful, away from the bustle. I can see why you enjoy it." Learning, Ada waiting for the servant girls to finish their obeisances and move on, arms laden with soiled linens. "Yes, the Imperial Palace sits in the middle of a lake fed by snowmelt in summer and frozen the rest of the year. The seraglio rests at the bottom of the palace, so beyond these walls is very cold water. Didn't you know?"

I hadn't. And, very likely, wasn't supposed to. Though surely my mother knew. And Saira and Jilliya, along with others who came from elsewhere, so it couldn't be *that* much of a secret. Still, I stored it away for possible future use. "Why worry about what lies outside our walls?" I asked with a smile. "Inside we are safe, warm, and fed. That's what's important."

She didn't reply immediately. When she spoke next, it was to exclaim over the painting on the wall beyond the little lagoon. "Why, it's brilliantly executed! May I?" When I nodded, she stepped closer and ran her fingers over the sunlit sea in the painting. Then she stepped back again, surveying from a greater distance. "Even knowing it's only a painting, my eye still sees it as a view out a window of a tropical sea going to the horizon. Amazing."

"See why we don't concern ourselves with what's beyond the wall? This water is much more pleasant."

She opened her mouth, then closed it firmly. "Certainly much more beautiful," she finally agreed.

"My apartments are up these stairs." I waved my hand for her to accompany me. "Over there are those of my mother, Her Imperial Majesty Empress Hulda. She is at court today, entertaining all of our guests. I hope your kind visit to us isn't taking you away from what I'm sure must be far more interesting activities."

"Far from it," Ada replied. "I am fortunate to gain this insight into the magic and beauty of the imperial seraglio—surely a once in a lifetime opportunity."

"Do you have a seraglio of such grandeur in Robsyn?" I inquired, feeling I should ask. Also I needed to prolong polite conversation long enough to send away Kaia and any servants who might be lingering.

"Oh, good Sól, no—we don't have one at all," Ada said in a rush, color high on her cheeks.

"Where do you live?" I asked, feeling as curious as Helva might ever be.

"Live? Well, Freddy and I share a set of rooms within the palace."

"How..." Odd. Invasive. Vulnerable. "Interesting," I finally supplied.

"Being in rooms by myself here is most strange," Ada said, as if agreeing. "I miss my husband, sleeping in my bed alone."

"Your servant girls would sleep with you if asked."

She made a wry moue. "They offered, but it's not the same as sleeping with your husband. I apologize—I'm realizing that you wouldn't know, of course."

No. And knowing what I did of Rodolf, I'd never be so foolish as to sleep in his presence. I'd wait for the security of the seraglio for that.

"Kaia!" I called, waking my nurse from her doze by the small fire in my sitting area. She jolted awake, her pained fingers clutching the throw she'd covered herself with. "I have a craving for svassnuht," I told her. "Would you make some for me? No one makes it like you do."

Kaia blinked muzzily. She'd been up as late as I, waiting for my return, then rose much earlier to attend to her usual duties. "Of course, Princess." She rose stiffly and shuffled out.

One by one, I summoned my other servants, sending them on various errands. When the last had cleared out, I turned to Ada. "In here is my bathing chamber." I dropped my voice. "We have a few moments before any return. What did you wish to tell me?"

Ada seemed somewhat astonished, gazing about. I hadn't asked her to sit, as I did not want any of the servants to suspect we'd have any sort of cozy conversation in their absence. Easy enough to sneak back to eavesdrop in that case. I led her to my bathing rooms, showing her the mother-of-pearl inlaid tub that had been a gift for my ninth birthday.

"Do the very walls have ears?" Ada asked softly.

"Yes, servants access our rooms from corridors and stairways at the back of the apartments," I replied, waving a hand at the carved lattice that made up the far wall. "That way they can come and go without disturbing us, but also be prepared to serve our least desire."

"So clever," Ada murmured.

"And see? I need only open this lever, to have hot water at any moment." I opened the tap so the water gushed noisily. Then guided Ada, with an insistent hand at her elbow, into my closet. Lined with cedar wood, it had no peep holes—that I'd ever found—and bordered none of the servants' passages. "Your confession?"

Ada blew out a breath. "I can see I don't have much time, so I'll be frank. Freddy asked me to befriend you, to insinuate myself into your company and wrangle an invitation to the seraglio, for the express purpose of creating a trust between us, to further our political interests."

I shouldn't feel this disappointment. My mother would laugh at me for having thought anything else, even for a moment. I was an imperial princess, which meant everyone would want my favor and influence. Mother had emphasized that enough times that I shouldn't feel so blindsided that Ada hadn't truly wanted to be my friend.

The abrupt sense of intense loneliness took me by surprise. A good lesson there.

"Oh! Please don't look so sad," Ada breathed, taking one of my hands in both of hers. "Curse being rushed that I put it so baldly. I only said it so because I wanted you to know that I very much like you and truly want to be your friend. I didn't want to continue on false pretenses, but I shouldn't have told you."

"Ah," was all I could think to say. Her hands gripped mine with a fervency I didn't quite understand.

"You don't believe me and I don't blame you. But let's pretend that you do, that you understand that if we'd known each other longer, we'd be fast friends and trust each other with everything. I'm sure that sounds impetuous to someone as poised and collected as you are."

I had to smile at that, amused she'd describe me thus. And yet... I understood what she was trying to say. I didn't think she'd be so clumsy if she'd planned this conversation. Unless she possessed a level of deviousness beyond even my experience with my mother.

"I'm willing to call us friends, yes. Now would you care to see—"

"Not yet." She held onto my hand and I looked at it pointedly. I wasn't accustomed to being handled so. *Better get used to it. Rodolf will do that and much worse*, a small voice whispered. "Jenna." Ada's voice went even lower and more urgent. "Do you need to be rescued?"

~ 9 ~

I gazed at her in astonishment. "Excuse me?"

"Oh, I'm doing this so badly. But this … marriage. Have you agreed to it?"

"Of course." I held up the hand she didn't have prisoner, showing her the hateful diamond. "You would not be here if I weren't getting married."

"That's not what I mean." She finally released my hand to press fingers to her temples. "You can't know, I know you're sequestered here, but that man. He has a reputation. A terrible one. It would take forever to—"

"Ada," I broke in. Enough of this. Time to put a stop to this before she worked herself into a frenzy worthy of one of Helva's tantrums. "I know about his previous wives. My brothers warned me."

Her mouth fell into an O, before she snapped it closed and searched my face. "Then you do know. So you must recognize that you cannot go through with this. Let me help you."

"Help me?" I nearly laughed, even as my heart hammered, my stomach turning over with a thousand feelings at once. "What will you do—have your Freddy stage a revolution to defy my father? For that is what it would take. And you're speaking to an imperial princess of treachery to the empire."

Her eyes flashed with anger. "How can you—"

"Your Imperial Highness? Did you plan to bathe or, oh! Forgive me." One of the servant girls bent in half with her apology. "The water, on the floor…"

I groaned at myself for such carelessness. "Oh that." I waved it away. "I simply forgot. The princessa wished to see my collection of Bøka silk klúts and we became absorbed. Clean it up."

"Immediately, Your Imperial Highness."

I regretted giving the girl extra, unnecessary work, but too late for it now. And it would keep her occupied. The rush of water shut off.

"Now this one," I told Ada, sliding open a drawer, "is also from Bøka, but from the southern region. Very rare."

She bent over to examine it and nodded. "Indeed." Then she glanced at me, expression full of concern. "I hate to see it locked away in a drawer."

"It's fine," I assured her. "It's stored as exactly as it's meant to be, according to plan."

"But will it survive harsh treatment?" she asked me, giving me a hard stare.

"That's not for me to say," I replied.

"I suppose not." Ada sounded as angry as she'd looked previously. "No matter how rare or valuable, a klút—even one of Bøka silk—is merely a thing, to be used and discarded, according the whims of its owner."

"Exactly," I agreed, walking away. "I'll escort you back out and show you some of the other treasures of our home along the way. Then Hede will show you back to your rooms so you may dress for the evening's festivities."

* * * *

My stomachache had gone to my head by the time I saw Ada off, paining me enough that I lay down for a while. I supposed the princessa had thought herself well-meaning, but she had no idea of what she proposed. That I might be able to refuse this marriage.

Rescue. From my own family, my own life. Impossible.

I fell asleep, hard and fast, and rose hours later feeling much more on balance. Much of my emotional state could be attributed to the short sleep of the night before—on top of all the excitement. I'd simply allowed myself to be overcome. I was the emperor's firstborn daughter, pearl of two great ruling families. Rodolf would not use me carelessly. His other wives must not have been so valuable. He would not dare harm me, for the same reasons I'd taunted Ada with. The subject kingdoms of the empire would never risk a reminder of their subjugation. No one could withstand the might of the Konyngrr fist.

Though I didn't want it, I ate the svassnuht Kaia brought me, so she wouldn't feel her efforts wasted. I wished I'd thought of an easier task for her. Truly, I wished I'd never arranged for Ada to speak to me privately. *Words that cannot be spoken aloud are not fit words for virtuous ears.* I understood that adage better than ever before.

I dressed in my dancing clothes with care, taking my time. At least I could be free of the elegant toenails, as I couldn't dance well in them. Besides which, Mother often observed that an imperial princess should not be confused with a skilled rekjabrel. I would not go to Rodolf as a dancing girl, but as a treasured wife. Just as I understood the basics of sexual intercourse and how to delight my husband, but not the finer points, as a virgin should not seem overly tutored. A man valued innocence in his wife, and I would bring that to our marriage.

Perhaps these other wives had disappointed him. Such a distinguished king would have high standards of behavior and comportment. If nothing else, my mother had trained me to an exquisite degree. I would not disappoint my husband, thus he'd never have any reason to abuse me. Mother had said many times—and conveyed through Kral the night before—that if I did my utmost, the Elskadyr family would reward me with power. They valued me and would protect me. Ada with her clumsy analogies simply didn't understand the ways of the great families.

I would please Rodolf exactly as I'd been raised to do, ensuring our happiness, and bearing him many heirs. Children to love. I should never have doubted—or allowed the whispered words of the princessa to give me pause. I would delight Rodolf in every way, beginning tonight with my dance.

* * * *

This time Inga stayed behind also, as it was my showcase, my night to shine alone, my mother declared. I missed Inga on the long walk through the eight doors. Unlocked, then locked again. The guards were all new ones tonight, and I missed those of the evening before.

Look at me, so childish as to cling to small bits of familiarity. Soon my entire life would change—for the better, as my family intended for me—so I must embrace the new and different.

It helped that I wore a long cloak, with a deep cowl over my head, as was traditional for this dance until the moment of reveal. Though made of ivory silk so light it floated, it kept me warmer than the revealing klút of the evening before. And its voluminous folds kept me hidden from those loathsome, too tactile gazes of the men.

Hestar did not arrive to escort me this time. He and everyone else awaited my performance in the grand hall. Instead, a line of rekjabrel dancers met me at the final door, escorted by a few guards. They wore diaphanous scarves, less than klúts, but nothing overtly sexual, nothing like what they normally wore for their dances for men. Tonight they served as a frame for my beauty, and would not dare distract from it.

Silently, they bowed in unison, graceful deep-knee bends, just as we'd practiced so many times in the dancing glen in the seraglio. They formed an oval around me, gliding with no sound, and we moved like mist to the grand hall. The guards stood at rigid attention, bowing to me before they opened the doors and we entered the hall.

I took my place at the center of the tiles, the rekjabrel swirling in a dance of tribute to the virgin bride, settling like flower petals around me.

All was silent but for the whisper of clothing as people shifted, a muffled cough from one. I took the moment to pray to the goddesses of women, to the three sisters—Glorianna, Moranu, and Danu—who governed the female provinces of love, beauty, and the quiet comforts of home.

Praying to embody perfect womanhood, I waited until the chimes, sweetly, whisper thin, the most fragile and delicate of melodies, trickled through the air. I allowed myself to sway to the music, finding the heart of it. Of course, I'd never been able to dance to music played by real musicians. All I'd had was the seraglio facsimile, the singing of women backed by the staccato beats and off-tune chimes of improvised instruments.

My mother had said it would be close enough, but that the real thing would be better. And she'd been right. Real music had an infectious glide, an implicit heart that seized mine and carried it. I made my first steps and the music followed.

Setting my bare feet carefully on the chill marble, I moved so my bells wouldn't chime. Not yet. The beginning was for innocence, for the silence of the meek and humble virgin bride. All they would see of me would be the occasional flash of my ankle, my toes—and then, the deliberate show of the arch of my foot.

Thus does the virgin seduce her husband, showing her tender, hidden aspects. See my naked ankle, my unveiled toes, the unscathed sole of my foot. I am untouched, gently raised in beauty, all to delight your senses.

I chanted the ancient poetry to myself as I danced, accelerating now as the music chased me, keeping my focus on the dance. If nothing else, I would execute this performance flawlessly. I would not shame my families or myself. All those dreams, those fantasies of the perfect husband, I poured them into the dance, showing my own longing and delight.

The cloak flared as my tempo increased, revealing my calves, and flashes of my knees and thighs. I threaded my hands through the folds, opening them like flowers, offering my palms, each cupping a large, lustrous pearl. A sigh ran through the room, a groan of desire, and this time I didn't mind, because I controlled it. I'd evoked it in them deliberately, stoking that fire with my dance, so carefully practiced and cultivated.

I moved faster, my upraised palms weaving, balancing the pearls in offering. The sway of my arms parted the cloak further, the glimpses of my body within tantalizing, then revealing. Sheer scarves draped me, held on by strings of tiny bells that chimed now that I allowed it. Otherwise I wore only pearls, glued on to cover my most intimate parts. Nothing but they and the dance obscured closer scrutiny.

And I didn't care. In fact, I loved it. I exulted in my power for this space of time, flaunting what they couldn't touch. I was beauty made flesh. All potent femininity, goddess, and exuberant youth, and whirling dance.

I spun, the cloak flaring wide and the hood falling back as I raised my face to the sky, to Sól, father of all light and life. I danced for the god. And for myself.

Without bobbling a pearl, I caught the last tie of the cloak with a pass of my hand, freeing it to fall at my feet. Loosed and unbound, my hair flew around me. It would stream to my ankles if I stopped moving.

But I never stopped moving. I accelerated, bells ringing loudly with the stomp of my feet and the flex of my body. I felt lithe and alive, taunting the musicians to keep up with me. They couldn't. No one could catch me unless I allowed it.

I whirled closer to the high table where the emperor sat with his heir and my future husband. Dim figures on the periphery of my dance. My blood sang and I simmered with power, holding them rapt in my spell.

With a final crash of drums, bells, and chimes, I folded at my future husband's feet, palms upraised and offering him the three pearls—one in each hand, and myself.

Perfectly executed.

Crashing applause broke the mesmerized silence, followed by cheers of excitement. My future husband plucked the pearls from my palms and said something I couldn't hear with the exhilaration so high in my ears, the roar of approval and admiration.

And I didn't care. He was a bit player in this. A mere observer to my exhibition of the epiphany of an imperial princess.

I remained where I was, gracefully crouched and shrouded by my hair, until the rekjabrel dancers swept up, wrapping me once again in the cloak, pulling the deep cowl over my head, and hiding me away. Rodolf might have plucked two pearls this night, but he'd wait one more for the third. I had one more day to be who I was, before I became something utterly other.

Do you need to be rescued?

As I walked back to the seraglio, allowing the bells their subtle music, I imagined what that might be like. In that moment, subsumed by the dance, it had seemed entirely possible that I could escape. I could soar away on the wings of the music and my own effervescent grace. With a sweep of my hand, I could scatter those men to the wind, laughing as I did so.

But with each door unlocked, opened, closed, and locked behind me, it seemed as if I left one more part of that woman behind. Until I finally entered the cloistered warmth of the seraglio, greeted by Hede's grave bow.

The lights dimmed for night, only a few women lingered here and there, the children all gone to bed, so the splash of waterfalls and murmured conversations were the only sounds. A group of rekjabrel passed, decked out for a night of sensual activity, their work just beginning, bowing deeply and murmuring compliments. They'd join my dancing companions to continue entertaining our guests. I wondered what Ada thought of all that.

Not ready to return yet to my apartments—especially to endure the trial of having the glued-on pearls soaked off, one by one—I gave my cloak to a servant and wandered over to the lagoon, for once still and undisturbed. Its glassy black surface shimmered under the moon-dim lights with glints of peach and orange. Would the real moon look like this—and would I get to see it, or was I trading one plush cage for another? The painters and artists made it look like a pearl, glowing white in a dark sky where they depicted the sun as burning yellow orange, in a field of startling blue.

Though I wanted to dip my now aching feet, I tucked them under me for the moment, unwilling to disturb the pristine surface. Bending over, I studied myself, a luminescent moon in that dark sky. I'd seen my clear reflection in the mirrors, of course, before I left for my dance. Making sure I'd missed no detail.

This image of me was different. Indistinct, a ghost of ivory white with shadows where her eyes should be. I looked, not exuberantly full of life and power, but already dead. A wraith of myself.

Which would it be for me, this marriage? Would I grasp the power promised me, become an empress to rule even my mother, or would I dissolve away into a memory. The lost princess, never to be seen or heard from again.

Do you need to be rescued?

No, I didn't require rescue, because I was an imperial princess. I would save myself. At least make an effort to take control, to seize the power I'd been promised. My mother shouldn't be surprised. After all, she'd created me.

Resolutely, I dropped my feet into the cool water, shattering that ghost self. In the morning, I'd confront my mother.

~ 10 ~

At our private breakfast—which Inga and Helva delayed until I woke up, quite late in the morning—my sisters were full of secondhand praise for my performance. The rekjabrel and other ladies in attendance had painted a glowing portrait of how well I'd done. Of course, no one had seen an imperial princess perform the ducerse dance, outside of practicing, since my mother had danced it for the emperor nearly two decades before. Many of the women weren't even that old.

Everyone had been dazzled.

"I hope I do that well, when it's my turn," Helva remarked wistfully. "I wish I could have seen you."

"If you want to do well, you'll have to get more dedicated about practicing," Inga observed, somewhat tartly. "And you have seen Jenna dance—hundreds of times, including the last weeks of dress rehearsals. It didn't look any different than what you've seen here."

Helva regarded me steadily. "I bet it did. That's what everyone is saying, that it was like Jenna became someone else. Is that how it felt?"

I couldn't see the harm in telling her. Or perhaps I'd grown less careful with my words, knowing what I'd go to that night. After all, what could my mother do to punish me that would be worse than handing me over to Rodolf? There was a freedom in that, facing the very worst.

"It did feel different, like the goddesses came to me, filled me with womanly power."

Helva sighed, a dreamy expression on her face, while Inga studied me with somewhat more cynicism. "Rumor is that you've requested an audience with your mother."

No secrets in the seraglio. I sipped my almond-milk sweetened tea. "I have. It's traditional for a bride to seek advice from her mother on her wedding day."

Inga nodded, studying her own tea, wrapping her hands around it. "Be careful, sister mine," she murmured.

Tempted to tell her I was beyond caring, I reached over and squeezed her hand. "Don't mourn me before I'm gone," I said, allowing my meaning to filter through it.

She turned her hand over, clutching mine in return. To my surprise, her lovely aqua eyes swam with tears. Helva looked between us, bewildered, and growing frightened. "What's wrong—what aren't you two telling me?"

"Nothing," I reassured her, releasing Inga's hand. "We're simply missing each other already."

"But we'll see you tomorrow morning," Helva said, almost a question in it. "You'll return here to sleep as all the noble ladies do, yes? At least until you travel to your new home. We have a week before we have to say goodbye." Her voice rose perilously and we shushed her.

"Of course you'll see me tomorrow morning," I said, forcing a smile. I couldn't imagine that Rodolf would part with that tradition and not allow me to return. The seraglio was our sanctuary, our refuge. The one place where men could not go. I would be back later tonight, no matter what else transpired.

Helva smiled with artless relief, oblivious to the undercurrents. "And you can tell us all about it, what it's really like."

Inga snorted. "You know what sex is about. Sól knows we've had countless lessons in the sensual arts."

"But that's all theory, with ivory implements. Don't you ever get the idea they're not telling us everything?" Helva insisted.

"If I did," Inga said reprovingly, "I would not be so foolish as to speak those words aloud."

Chastened, Helva subsided, picking sullenly at her disassembled pastry.

"Your Imperial Highness Princess Jenna," Hede said from behind me, bowing when I turned. "Her Imperial Majesty will receive you now."

"Thank you, Hede." I rose, making sure to first wipe my lips of any crumbs. I'd dressed for breakfast, and had my girls fix my hair in a casual style, in anticipation that she'd call me early. The afternoon would be filled with preparations for the wedding ceremony.

"Good luck," Inga said, catching and holding my gaze.

I nodded. I would need all the good fortune I could capture.

* * * *

"Ah, here she is. The beautiful bride, pearl of the empire," my mother commented when her girl ushered me in. Something in her tone smacked of sarcasm—or envy, perhaps—but for my mother, she sounded almost cheerful.

"Your Imperial Majesty." I spoke as reverently as I could muster, sinking into a deep curtsey, calling on my dancer's grace, as I knew it would please her.

"Sit." She gestured to the pillows opposite her low table. "Have some tea."

I'd long since learned that my mother's "tea" was actually mjed, and not watered down. Women weren't supposed to drink mjed, as the fiery brew would overbalance our more delicate, watery constitutions, but few rules applied to the empress. And she would think me weak if I refused. So, despite the early hour, I allowed her girl to pour me a cup, and sipped from it, the fiery honey liquor a welcome burn.

"You've done very well," mother said. Though her beautifully angled face remained impassive and icy, the compliment warmed me. Her opos pipe sat quietly. She would not smoke her opos until later that night, only when she'd returned to the seraglio for the evening and could afford to set aside her formidable wits. "Better than I expected. Your dancing was without flaw. Both His Imperial Majesty and His Highness King Rodolf are more than impressed with you. Your father is proud and your future husband utterly besotted. Even your brothers were dazzled."

She sounded dry, a hint of scorn in her voice despite the compliments. But I thanked her as graciously as I could.

"Tonight you wed Rodolf," she continued, unbending a bit as her girls apparently disappeared. She held all her servants in an iron grip of discipline and fear, making this room relatively safe for sharing secrets. No one—including me—had the spine to betray her in even the smallest gesture. "At last everything you've worked for is within your grasp. Tomorrow you'll be a queen and set your feet on the next step of our journey to restoring our family to glory."

I took a breath. Let it out. Perhaps I didn't dare say anything. Certainly I couldn't confess my fear.

"What is it?" she prodded impatiently. "Surely this wasn't a surprise. You knew I hoped to secure the King of Arynherk for you."

"Yes, Mother." I'd gone shivering and timid, as I always did in her presence. In this room where she'd taught me the brutal lessons of obedience and the price for failing her. "Though he is somewhat other than I expected."

She laughed, not cruelly, but in genuine amusement. "Don't tell me you had some girlish fantasy of prince charming—someone young and handsome who might kiss your feet and worship at your innocent loins? Oh, yes, I can see you did. How odd. I can't imagine how I could have gone so wrong. I thought you were smart enough to understand that this marriage is not for some poetic ideal of love but for the only thing that's real in this world: power."

I did understand that. I hadn't expected love. But I had thought my husband would be someone I wouldn't fear with gut-watering dread.

"Remember, too," she continued, "the great advantage of an elderly husband. I have given you a tremendous gift which you seem to lack the wit to recognize. He surely cannot live many more years. You will outlast him, if you're not a fool about it, and then you will be a widow—both free of him and in possession of all he owns. We have planned all of this with exquisite care. Trust in that."

"Yes, Mother." It made sense. If only I *could* outlast him. "But there are rumors."

"There are always rumors in the seraglio," she scoffed. "It is the lifeblood that warms the waters and brightens the lives of fools with nothing better to think about. Are you one of those empty-minded idiots who gives credence to every whisper and innuendo?"

Of course, I didn't dare reveal my source. My mother—and possibly the emperor—would deal harshly with my little brothers for their well-intentioned warnings. "No, Mother," I replied, casting about for my next step. I'd had such bold speeches planned, but they'd all fled from my mind.

"Of course not," she replied, most satisfied. "For you are my daughter, through and through. This is a brilliant match for you. We are so close, my darling girl. Don't lose heart now."

Her words made me look up, feeling somewhat encouraged, and I fancied I glimpsed something of sympathy in her face. "We all endure," she said softly. "That is the woman's burden in this world. We must endure the pawings of men, for only through them can we express our power. I wish it could be otherwise—believe me, you have no idea how much I wish it so—but it's simply not. This is the way of things. If you stay here, an eternal virgin, safe and warm among other women, you will never be anything more than you are. A waste of all your promise. With your beauty, talent, intelligence, and fortitude, you can become the most powerful woman in the world. But not by staying here."

I stared at her, rapt. She'd never been so honest with me. Nor so complimentary. She gave me a wry smile, and poured us both more mjed, a rare gesture for her, to do it herself. "Tell me what rumors have unsettled you."

No slithering out of that one. She'd know if I lied and she'd never relent until I confessed. "I've heard his four previous wives all died, very young."

She shrugged, as if that mattered not at all. "True. Rodolf has a reputation for being ... *hard* on his brides." She smiled without mirth, blue eyes drilling into me. "Do you imagine yourself so easily broken?"

I hadn't thought of it that way. She leaned in, a glimpse of teeth before she closed her lips over them. The opos smoke had stained her teeth over the years, despite the many remedies she attempted and commanded her girls to discover. She'd developed the closed-lipped smile to hide them, reminding me ever of that jeweled lizard I'd loved, even after it bit me.

"You are of my body," she said, deep blue eyes intent on mine. "More, you are trained by me. Did you imagine I taught you pain for no reason? I have crafted you from my flesh and molded you with my will. What can Rodolf do to you that you have not already withstood? Nothing." She sat back, eyes going to her pipe, fingers twitching for it, before she mastered the urge and tapped her nails on the cup of mjed instead. "Besides, you are an imperial princess. He won't dare to kill you as he did the others. Your father is intensely pleased with you—I take credit for that, but you deserve some as well—and as long as you behave impeccably, he'll continue to regard you as a priceless treasure. Keep on your father's good side, and your life will be safe."

And my body? I dared not speak that aloud.

"Jenna," my mother said, calling me by my name, as she so rarely did. My father had chosen it and it was not an Elskadyr name, something that rankled in her. "On this, your wedding day, I'll let you in on one last secret. For all that we've taught you the sensual arts to practice, they are largely unnecessary. It's easy for a woman, because she needs only submit to her husband's lust. Meekly accept what he wishes to do to you, and remember that it's only flesh. *You* are your mind and your will. That cannot be broken unless you are so weak as to allow it. And you, my pearl, are not weak, are you?"

"No, Mother, I'm not." I met her gaze, feeling a slow burn of anger somewhere near my heart. She returned the stare, a flicker of something else in it.

"I'm glad to hear it," she replied. "Your obedience does honor to your family. Now, go prepare for your wedding."

* * * *

The actual wedding ceremony, the ritual that bound me forever into Rodolf's possession, lasted a very short time. Not that there hadn't been days of contract negotiations and various ceremonies to solemnize my transference from my father's responsibility to Rodolf's, but my presence at those had been unnecessary.

For a woman without protection, without a father or brothers to speak for her and look after her best interests, such negotiations can work badly against her. Such women often become rekjabrel or lower servants. I've heard tales and they are hair-raising indeed. So, the audience with my mother had provided some comfort after all. No reprieve from my fate, but I'd hardly dared even entertain a flicker of hope for that. Instead, she'd reminded me that I am not alone in this world. I have a family who treasures me and cares for my well-being.

The emperor would see to it that his gift to Rodolf would be well looked after. I needed to trust in that.

So, the role I played in my own wedding was a small one. Hours of dressing and being decorated led me to a scant few minutes. My father, the emperor himself, performed the final ceremony. He lifted my veils, smiling broadly, and kissed me on the forehead. The first and last kiss I received from my father. Turning me to Rodolf, he presented me, waiting for my husband's formal acknowledgment of my identity. Dasnarian tales are rife with such trickeries, with other women, or even farm animals substituted for the promised bride.

But then, there are also tales of vows of eternal and undying love. Of lovers pledging themselves to each other, refusing the wishes of their families, running off together to live in happiness in mythical lands. Those are obviously also nothing but stories as absurd as those about men accidentally marrying sheep disguised as brides.

Making his promises to care for me, to give me food and shelter, to honor me as first wife and Queen of Arynherk, Rodolf fastened the wedding bracelets on me. Like the betrothal ring, the bracelets were old, prized jewels of the Arynherk kingdom and his ruling family. Wrapped in gold and silver, encrusted with diamonds, they weighed on me as heavy as the ring, which attached to the bracelet on my right hand with a set of three chains—gold, silver, and iron—delicately wrought and symbolic of my binding.

Fortunately, I didn't need to speak, only accept the bracelets and fastening of the chains. If I'd been required to speak, to vocalize my acceptance of this man, whose very proximity made my skin crawl with phantom spiders, I might not have gotten through it. As it was, I retreated into that cool bubble inside myself, the space my mother had taught me to develop and refine. Once inside, I felt nothing. I could be the pearl on the surface, shimmering and without blemish, passed from one hand to another.

The final ceremony, of course, would be when my husband claimed my virginity, making my body his and his alone. Thus we went directly from the marriage binding to his bedchamber. There would be a party for me the next day, in the seraglio, to celebrate my passage into womanhood. Inga and Helva had it all planned, keeping the details secret in their delight. I only knew they'd invited Ada and a few other visiting ladies, too.

I hadn't decided how I felt about speaking with Ada again. I'd spotted her in the wedding gathering. But when we had an opportunity to speak again, I would be Rodolf's wife in every way, so her seeds of doubt would find no purchase in my mind.

Besides which, I had taken refuge in thinking of nothing. That allowed me to be as meek as my mother dictated, my hand wrapped through the crook of Rodolf's arm as he led me to his grand chambers, his hand hot and damp with sweat as it covered mine. He breathed in short bursts of lustful excitement, and I briefly entertained an enticing wish that he might expire as he plowed my body and attempted to plant his seed.

A happy thought, as I might end up a queen, a mother, and a widow for one night of trouble. *If only.*

We entered his rooms, grand and foreign to my eye. The rekjabrel had described the beds the men slept in, but my mind's eye hadn't painted them exactly. Nothing like our silk-draped couches and piles of pillows, this bed loomed with masculine presence, large and straight-lined, bordered by posts at the four corners.

The servant girls that accompanied us relieved me of my veils and the heavily brocaded overdress of ivory satin decorated with a fortune in pearls. They carried it off, closing the door as Rodolf commanded, leaving me in only the transparent wisp of a sheath, and the dubious shield of my unbound hair. I kept my face averted and my eyes closed, grateful for the custom that allowed me to avoid looking at him.

Grateful, too, perhaps for my mother's harsh training over the years, that enabled me to remain rooted to the spot, despite the instincts that urged me to run as far and fast as I could.

But I couldn't contain my trembling. All that kept me from voiding my bladder in all that old remembered terror was that I hadn't eaten or drunk more than bare sips of water since lunch the day before. Fasting made me clean inside and out, for whatever orifice my husband wished to take. And

I could only be glad for the women who'd gone before me, in their wisdom in keeping the bladder empty, too.

I would submit, but at least I would not humiliate myself in that way.

Rodolf ripped the delicate silk from me, tossing the shift into the fire, then stirring the dregs to make sure it burnt completely. I would be naked until he clothed me. He returned to me, walking around me, looking and making little grunts of delight. I cracked my eyes open enough to track his movements, so I'd be ready for whatever came next.

He'd shed his own robe, his corpulent flesh jiggling rather unpleasantly as he circled me. Beneath his prodigious belly, his rather less than prodigious manhood remained flaccid, not at all aroused enough to perform the deed required. To be truthful, it didn't look large enough to penetrate my body and plant his seed—nothing like the illustrations—though I knew from lessons that it should increase in length considerably, once aroused.

With some men, being with a woman, seeing her naked, that was enough. Others required more stimulation.

Thus, when Rodolf wrapped his fist in my hair and forced me to my knees, I wasn't surprised. I'd practiced this, on carved phalluses, and set to work—steeling my stomach against the stink of him. He kept up the grunting, thrusting against me so his belly smacked my forehead, making it difficult for me to stay in position. I slid my hands up his legs, keeping my touch sensual as I'd been taught, hoping to use the leverage for purchase.

Wrong move. With a cry of rage, he backhanded me. I fell to the plush carpet, recovering my senses.

"You do what I tell you, wife," he growled. Seizing me by the rope of my hair, he dragged me to the bed. Though I tried hard not to resist, he yanked me off balance, making it difficult to keep up. He hauled me to my feet and fastened my wedding bracelets to a chain dangling from one of the crosspieces. My toes barely touched, the metal cutting into my wrists.

Now he fondled me, hands clammy soft and also surprisingly painful in their pinching. Though I tried to remain pliant, I couldn't help flinching away now and again. When I cried out, he laughed. And his manhood finally lengthened.

So, that is how it would be.

"So sensitive," he mused. "All of this lovely skin for me to learn and use against you for my pleasure. You'll learn discipline from me, *imperial princess*. Let's start with a little whipping."

After that, it only got worse.

~ 11 ~

Do you need to be rescued?

The question seeped through and around in my dreams. Dreams of pain, suffering, and humiliation such as I'd never anticipated. When I'd first collapsed into sleep—when Rodolf had finally tired of me and sent me home to the seraglio—I'd seized the bliss of unconsciousness with profound gratitude.

Then the dreams came, replaying the events of my wedding night, throwing me awake again and again. Every time I awoke, flailing to escape, sometimes on a scream, Kaia would be there offering me the gryth tea. Changing the compresses on my bruises.

This time, though, Kaia slept on the pillows beside me, a damp cloth still clutched in her crooked fingers, her face slack with exhaustion. She'd stayed awake all night to tend me. A burst of feeling made tears leak from my eyes. Kaia had always been so good to me. Perhaps I could arrange for her to retire as Old Mara had, once I left.

My stomach curdled and I nearly vomited at the thought. Rodolf might have to keep me alive, but I had no doubt I'd come to sorely regret that I'd have no recourse into death. Those other wives…perhaps he hadn't killed them, after all. They might have found a way to suicide.

Who could blame them?

The room remained dim, the light and heavy curtains all drawn, but sound filtered in from the seraglio. Music and clattering of dishes. The party. To celebrate my wedding.

I stared up at the silk-draped ceiling, the one I'd been looking at all my life—or at least since I was five and old enough to rate my own apartments. It seemed impossible to consider moving, to lever myself out of bed, much less face any of them. I ached in every pore, and with screamingly acute pain in some places I didn't want to think about. Places that Rodolf had... *Don't think about it.*

My wrists hurt, throbbing with it, the wedding bracelets cutting in painfully, so I lifted my hands to look. Kaia must have been the one to bandage them, carefully wrapping the skin beneath the bracelets, but she hadn't been able to remove the locked-on bracelets themselves, of course. Nor could she have cleaned all the blood that caked in and around the sparkling gems. Not that the jewels cared. They caught and scattered the scant light regardless, coldly uncaring about the woman who wore them.

If my mother had offered me a draught of poison at that moment, I would have taken it.

As if on cue, the curtains thrust open, and the empress stood there, staring down at us. Kaia awoke with a squeak and a start, cowering off the bed by pure instinct. Only the second time my mother had come to my bedchamber, and I didn't miss the parallel. Both times I'd been sick, weak, and terrorized. My mother heaved an exasperated sigh. "Get up," she snapped. "Get her up and bathed," she instructed her girls and mine, who hovered behind her, eyes wide and faces pale. "You're late for your wedding celebration."

"I can't—" I barely managed, my voice hoarse from the screaming and weeping I'd eventually succumbed to.

"You can and you will. You're an imperial princess, Queen of Arynherk. Show some dignity. Do you want everyone to know how weak you are?"

They knew already. They had to know. No secrets in the seraglio. Women talked, particularly about the cruel men, the sadistic ones and those with odd bents. The rekjabrel traded with each other when they could, those who could extract sexual pleasure from pain more willing to go to those types. But it seemed a truth that the truly cruel men preferred women who hated it, taking as much pleasure in forcing them to suffer as in their own sexual excitement.

I'd seen it in Rodolf. Once I'd stopped trying to submit gracefully, he'd begun to truly enjoy himself. A lesson there, I supposed. No sense in withholding my tears and cries of pain, as he'd keep going until he broke them out of me.

The girls helped me to sit, hurting me despite how carefully they placed their hands, while another turned on the hot tap in my bathing chamber. I was still naked, as Rodolf had only given me a cloak to wrap up in for the journey back to the seraglio. The male guards had even been kind to me, so I must have looked horrible. One from the third set of doors picked me up and carried me as far as he could, before he turned me over to the women guards.

And Hede, of all people, she'd met me at the top of the stairs to the seraglio with a litter, settling me on it and helping to carry it, along with her strongest ladies, so I didn't have to descend on my own power. She'd known before the fact, and I didn't question how. Hede might be our enforcer, but she also looked after the rekjabrel. She'd know which men created the most damage.

I yelped as the hot water stung in a hundred places, most of all between my legs. My mother didn't watch as the girls helped me, unwinding the bandages so I could be cleaned. Instead she perused my closet, returning with a klút and several complimentary and contrasting scarves. Not the festive klút I'd planned to wear for my party, but a much longer one, more sedate.

"You'll learn to cover the marks," my mother informed me, not unkindly. Maybe even with a sort of sympathy, under it all. "Longer klúts that you can drape to both cover yourself and to be loose enough not to bind you uncomfortably. The scarves will assist to cover what the klút won't. Did he at least spill his seed in your woman's passage?"

I nodded wearily, unwilling to revisit the implements he'd gleefully used to insert the seed he spilled elsewhere.

"Good. Once you're with child, you can refuse him. If you pay attention to your cycles, that can give you eight months of respite."

It made sense, all of a sudden, why Jilliya kept conceiving babies. Though each pregnancy, each miscarriage weakened her, she always sought to conceive again. Could that be why? Was it possible that our father also treated his wives as... With a shudder that became a wracking convulsion, I thrust that image away also, tears suddenly pouring down my face.

"Give her my tea," my mother said, and her favorite girl, Petra, was there, holding the mug to my lips, cupping my head to steady it, crooning encouragement, her dark eyes kind. I drank, nearly choking on the strength of the mjed combined with the much stronger than usual gryth tea. She kept feeding it to me in sips, the languid numbing of the liquor and analgesic combining to make me float in the hot water. It finally penetrated to my bones, and I stopped shivering.

The girls emptied the tub, the pink-tinged water sluicing away, and they added more while I sat in it. Had it only been two days before that I showed Ada how the tub worked? I thought I'd been afraid then. *Do you need to be rescued?* Maybe if I'd known then what I know now...

But nothing had truly changed, not in my chances of escaping this fate. My mother studied my every bruise, swelling, and laceration, instructing the girls in how to treat them—how to best numb and conceal my injuries. She set one to soaking my wedding bracelets in a bowl of water, meticulously working with a small brush to liberate the sparkling gems of my blood and other more unseemly substances. Another was tasked to sew padding to fit inside the bracelets, to be ready for that evening.

"If he's going to string you up by the wrists," my mother commented to me, "some padding will help to reduce the damage to your skin. But smarter for you not to make him do it."

I didn't reply to that and for once she didn't require an answer. She might have known how empty that advice was. When they finally had me as clean as possible, and I drifted on a cloud of delightful nothingness, they wrapped my hair in a towel and helped me out of the tub, and into a cushioned chair. At my mother's detailed instruction, they used makeup to cover any of the wounds that might show beyond the concealing klút and scarves. My face received most of her attention.

Though they'd put a cold compress on the swelling around my eye and on my cheekbone, it had only helped so much. My mother studied it, frowning. "I'm going to have to speak to the emperor to caution your husband to stay clear of your face. It won't do for you to leave the Imperial Palace looking as if you've been beaten."

I laughed, the pitch rising into hysterical, and she gave me her coldest, meanest stare. It slid off of me. My mother no longer frightened me, as I'd met a far worse monster.

"Get a handle on yourself," she commanded. "You're stronger than this. Better than this. Sure, he beat you a little. Welcome to being a woman. It's only flesh. You'll heal. And one day he'll be dead and you can dance on his grave all you like. Now pay attention to your makeup. Before long you'll have to teach your new servant girls how to do this." She glared at her girl. "Or, as it appears Rodolf loses all sense in his lust, I might have to send Petra with you."

Petra facing away from my mother, widened her eyes slightly. Hope? I'm sure serving the empress would be no leisure day, but could Petra actually wish to leave the Imperial Palace? I dug some words out of my sluggish brain. "That might be helpful if she came with me."

Dabbing the makeup around my tender eye, so gentle it barely stung, Petra gave me a slight smile. Well then.

They styled my hair so it fell around the injured side of my face, dressed me and decked me with scarves and jewels. I didn't much care. I'd drunk enough of Mother's tea that I no longer cared about anything. They carried me down in a chair bedecked with trailing flowers, a wedding celebration custom I'd never connected to the fact that the bride might be in such pain between her legs that she could barely stand, much less walk.

I'd paid little attention to the other custom, of mothers attending their daughters the morning after losing their virginity. Even the rekjabrel had such traditions, as a virgin rekjabrel was highly sought by some men and the occasion of her transition into womanhood always a noteworthy event. Never had I expected my own mother to lower herself to such a lowbrow custom, though now I understood the purpose.

They'd carefully tutored us in how to pleasure men and the basics of sexual interludes of all types, but they'd left out the pain and terror of it. No wonder. If we'd known, the young women would refuse to ever leave the seraglio.

As I surveyed the crowd of women cheering my arrival as they carried me down the short flight of stairs from my apartments, I scanned the crowd of women. What would the men do, if we barricaded the doors and refused to come out? They might violate the sanctity of the seraglio, batter down the doors and drag us out again. We couldn't fight them, with their strength and their weapons.

But it wouldn't take so much as that, it suddenly occurred to me. I scanned the walls, beautifully painted with their vistas that tricked the eye, and remembered how Ada had said that beyond them lay freezing water. Some fruit grew in the seraglio, under our enchanted suns, but most of it came from outside, carried in by servant girls. They could starve us out in no time.

Ridiculous of me to entertain, even for a moment, that we could... what—rebel? Laughable.

Still, as they situated me at the head of the feast table, I spotted Ada nearby. Not close enough to speak to me, but near enough for me to catch her uneasy pallor as she studied me, the pain in her gaze. I looked away, accepting the congratulations of Saira and Jilliya, who'd stirred themselves for this occasion—no doubt at my mother's command.

Inga and Helva were there, too, of course. All the women of the seraglio were, with the exception of servants needed for critical duties in the palace. They'd been given a few leisure hours to attend my party, and all who could had taken advantage of the opportunity.

All of this makes it sound as if I were aware and observant, which I was not. That day is a blur to me, as are the ensuing days. I don't remember any conversations. Truly I don't remember much of the pain, except in an abstract way. I believe I never spoke directly with Ada again. If Helva and Inga said anything to me, I don't recall it.

I drank a great deal of Mother's tea, and—that evening when I broke down into hysterics when they attempted to dress me for another visit to my husband—Mother had her servants carry in her pipe. She taught me how to slowly inhale the opos smoke, and to hold it deep in my lungs, until the bone-melting properties invaded deep enough that I could let it go.

The dreaminess it created didn't outlast my husband's extended attentions, but it allowed me to abandon pride sooner, giving him the tears, cries, and pleas that so worked to excite his lust.

I believe it was the fourth evening after my wedding that I broke entirely. Even I didn't see it coming, but as I walked to the doors in my dreaming haze of pleasant numbness, I lost all control and tried to run. Hede had to chase me down and eventually tie me to the litter to be carried—gagged so the screaming wouldn't disturb anyone else—to my husband's chambers. A development that delighted him.

He loved nothing so well as my fear, and my mother chastised me for being so weak as to give him that weapon against me.

At least he never damaged my face again. Such was my father's service in protecting me.

~ 12 ~

Exactly a week after I first left the seraglio, I prepared to exit it forever. One more formal reception, to give our farewells, and I would leave the Imperial Palace for my new home.

There, of course, had not been days of savoring time with Helva and Inga and my other friends among the ladies. When allowed to, I'd spent my time sleeping in murky kaleidoscopic dreams, or soaking in hot water with numbing and healing herbs. Rodolf had backed off somewhat in afflicting new marks on the skin he so prized. The sight of my existing lash marks and the always seeping wounds under my wedding bracelets—despite the clever padding within—served well enough to excite him.

For my first appearance outside the seraglio since my wedding, my mother had caused the ladies to fashion me long silk gloves to slide on under the bracelets. Fingerless, they allowed my diamond ring to show, and fastened with a hook under the chains that attached the ring to my bracelet. Studded with pearls in swirling designs, the gloves covered my arms up to the drape of my klút in clever concealment.

Inga was allowed to come with me again, but Helva didn't even make a token protest about wanting to attend. She'd taken to watching me with wild, horrified eyes, then avoiding me altogether. I saw Saira counseling her in quiet nooks several times. They would have a challenge there, in getting Helva to joyfully greet whatever husband the emperor chose for her. Not that her joy, or lack thereof, would matter in the least so far as changing her fate. Perhaps she'd get luckier than I.

Mother wouldn't let me have the opos smoke before the reception, as she declared it unseemly for me to have it on my breath. I thought she worried what I might say, in my uncaring haze. She actually bribed me with it, in exchange for my good behavior, that I might have it that evening when I returned to the seraglio, and take a pipe with me in my trousseau, along with a goodly supply of opos for future use. Petra would go with me—another wedding gift—and she knew how to keep me supplied.

We'd come to a strange new rearrangement, that my mother bribed instead of bullied me. She likely recognized how she'd been so thoroughly supplanted in commanding me through suffering.

I didn't even question how Petra, a servant girl in a kingdom that would be completely foreign to us both, would arrange to supply me with opos. At that point I only cared that she would. Or, perhaps it would be more accurate to say that I cared about nothing at all as long as I could hide behind the smoke haze.

Maybe not even then.

When we emerged from the final door, Hestar appeared to escort Inga this time, and my husband to escort me. It seemed so odd to see Rodolf clothed and wearing a mask of civility. He kissed my hand, admiring my gloves, and tucked my arm through his, speaking genially of my beauty and grace, and how I'd enjoy the journey to Arynherk on the morrow.

Though I cowered internally at his least movement, I found myself studying him from the corners of my lowered gaze. It disturbed me deeply, to reconcile this king with his fine clothing, iron crown, and perfect manners, with the brute who took savage delight in debasing me. I felt as if I'd entered some other realm I didn't understand. Not surprising, as even without the opos smoke fogging my mind, it left a dreamy residue behind.

Sometimes I thought I might be dreaming, that I'd awaken from some feverish nightmare, having concocted all of it.

The reception was smaller, more intimate, the visitors from both near and far having returned to their homes. This last evening was for family and our intimates. The emperor, Hestar at his side, gave a speech and a toast, wishing me happiness in my new life. I had to be nudged to drink from my glass of light wine. A special treat for me and Inga, and the few other noble ladies present, to indulge in it. Something that amused me greatly, having been initiated into the far stronger alcohol and numbing drugs the ladies used to ease the pain of wifely existence.

Neither my father nor Hestar paid me any attention beyond that toast. I'd already ceased to exist in their minds, like a piece of land sold for a tidy profit. Their minds and conversations turned to other matters. Rodolf excused himself to go speak with them, explaining to me that he should employ all his remaining time in the Imperial Palace bending the emperor's ear. Wary of his pretty manners, I only heard that he would not summon me that night, in order to spend the most time solidifying certain commitments. And so that I could rest for the journey.

After which I'd be isolated from even the meager protection my family had afforded me.

Wanting only to excuse myself to return to the seraglio, so I could sleep and savor the sweet reprieve of these last few hours, I considered my options for leaving. Inga, however, would not want to go, and she had fallen into fast conversation with Kral.

Though it seemed they spoke about me, as he looked over her head at me with narrowed eyes. He shook his head at her—then shrugged off her staying hand, though he didn't step away, instead bending to say something to her in rapid, hissed words. Our other brothers ringed behind him, not paying attention to their conversation at all, if they could even have overheard amid the general hubub. Leo, Loke and Mykal laughed over some joke. And Harlan's serious gray eyes rested on me.

I lowered my gaze quickly, but before I could duck away, he came over, bowing deeply. "We have the same salon set aside, Sister," he said gravely, "if you'd like to join us for some conversation, as before."

"Thank you, but no," I replied softly. I couldn't imagine enduring that, with myself some broken thing compared to the week before.

He frowned at me, raising his hand, and I flinched. "Jenna." His voice was full of many things. Too many for me to sort, except I could pick out the pity, the same that had been in his eyes. I had been reduced to a thing to be pitied. Slowly he took my hand in both of his, examining the ring and wedding bracelets, fingers skimming over the silk gloves, as if he guessed at what lay beneath.

"How can I help you?" he asked, in a tone so quiet I might have imagined I heard it. *Do you need to be rescued?*

I glanced up at him, maybe to check to see if I'd hallucinated the words—another fragment of drugged dreams—and caught him studying the fading bruise on my cheek. The makeup very nearly concealed it, but only very nearly. I averted my face, turning it so he couldn't see. Too late and too careless.

"Did Rodolf hit you?" Harlan asked, anger threading through his deep voice, enough that it cracked a little, the adolescent boy surfacing in his upset.

I laughed, the breathy crawl just short of hysteria that had become my new laugh. If he only knew. That backhand to my face—the first blow Rodolf gave me, a twisted bit of nostalgia there—had been the very least of what he'd done to me. But all of that was so carefully hidden away beneath my clothes, the subtle and diligent art of the seraglio.

Across the room, my mother watched us, eyes sharp and the warning clear in her face. So I summoned a smile for my baby brother. "A lapse in agility on my part. There's no cause for concern."

He clearly didn't believe me, his expression so transparently incredulous that I shifted a bit, making him turn so his back presented more fully to my mother.

"Why would you lie?" Harlan demanded. "Our father needs to know. We can't let you leave with that—"

"Hush!" I cut in, for his voice had risen too loud in his indignation. So like his full sister Helva in his way, with their impetuous naiveté. "Take me to this salon."

He offered an arm, escorting me, his rage palpable through the flexing of his forearm. My mother tracked us with an intent stare and I knew we'd only have a moment or two. Once inside the little grouping of chairs, Harlan moved to pull the curtains, but I stopped him. I'd rather keep an eye on who might listen in. In fact, there went a young page from Mother to Kral, who immediately turned from Inga to attend the empress.

"Jenna, you have to tell—" Harlan began, and I rounded on him.

"You're a fool," I shot the quiet words at him. Whispers are easier to overhear, so I kept my voice velvety soft. "You're only a boy so it's understandable, but you will say nothing to anyone."

He stared at me, completely taken aback. "You're hurt. I could feel it when you walked. What has he done to you? Don't tell me you enjoy it, because I see in your eyes how—"

"Don't say it." I nearly sobbed it. Kral looked our direction, our mother speaking in his ear. "It doesn't matter because they already know. My mother intervened—and our father made sure my face wouldn't be damaged again." And that only while I might be publicly viewed. Rodolf had promised that would change, since my pretty face mattered so much to me that I'd have the emperor himself chastise him for it.

"They … know?" Harlan echoed in disbelief, some of that innocence dying in his eyes as he processed that information. Behind him, Kral cut through the crowd like the shark he was named for, face hard and eyes sharp on me.

"Yes. And you can't do anything about it. They'll only punish you. Forget me. If you want to do something for me, treat your women well in my memory." My eyes filled with tears, but I lowered my gaze and blinked them back.

"Sister," Kral spoke, coming up on Harlan's flank and edging him aside. "Our mother sends her regards and notes that you have an early start tomorrow. It's best that you return to the seraglio to rest. I'll escort you." He offered an arm and I took it.

"Jenna," Harlan said, sounding torn between frustration and desolation.

Kral paused, giving him a searing glare. "Stay out of this, little rabbit. You've already drawn attention and you know what happens to all of us then. Say goodbye to Jenna."

"We already did. Have a good life, Harlan. That's what I wish for you, baby brother." Firmly turning my back on him, I allowed Kral to escort me swiftly out the doors and into the long hall that led through the main part of the Imperial Palace. I'd never even seen all of it.

"Our mother is concerned that you'll jeopardize this very important alliance," Kral said, looking straight ahead, a bulge in his jaw. I wondered what needles our mother used to keep him on her leash.

"I won't," I replied, not even bothering to be angry or offended. Unlike Harlan, Kral possessed little ability to see what anyone else suffered. I doubted he'd even thought of me as anything but a game piece, a bynd from the game we'd played as children to sacrifice in order to improve his chances at the throne. "I've gone along with everything."

"You could make an effort to look happier," he grunted. "A new bride should be radiant with joy."

I laughed at that, my twisted, mostly hysterical one, and he looked down at me, maybe actually seeing me for once.

"Is there a reason you're not happy?" He asked. "Besides having a selfish temper tantrum about not wanting to leave the Imperial Palace."

Ah, that was my mother's explanation. Plausible enough, I supposed, to explain to a young man not yet my age. Still, if I said nothing at this point, it made me complicit in my own terrorizing. Something about Harlan's astonishment at my easy capitulation stuck with me. But could I break a lifetime of obedience?

"If I said I didn't want to go," I breathed, "would you help me?"

Kral jerked his head back, firming his lips together. "You have to go with your husband. That is the way of things, no matter your feminine worries."

I nodded, beyond weary. I'd expected that answer.

Kral patted my hand, not seeming to notice the gloves at all. "You'll grow accustomed to your new home. Your husband is wealthy and you'll want for nothing. It's a good life. And we'll be working behind the scenes, putting the pieces in place."

I knew without a doubt that he hoped to supplant Hestar as heir. It showed in the ambitious light in his icy eyes as he winked at me. The pair of us, pretending we colluded with such wit when Kral would be as much a bynd as I in our mother's game. Though he'd enjoy a considerably better life while he did.

"Truly," he said, as we ascended the curving stairs, his voice very low, "your role—while critical and you'll always have my gratitude for it—is the easy one. You need only enjoy your life of leisure while I work on my part. Surely you can do that much?"

A life of leisure. I hadn't thought I'd harbored any hope, and yet I must have because it sank like a stone from my heart and through my stomach. Would my death upset their plans? Probably so, if I suicided, but not if I kept Rodolf happy and sealed to the Elskadyr cause. Though, if he killed me—say by accident during his idea of sex—then he might feel enough remorse to continue to support the Elskadyrs against the emperor and Hestar, should it come to that. In fact, if he killed me, then my father might hold Rodolf to account, giving him a reason to fight back—with the Elskadyrs and their allies turning the surprise by supporting him.

My mother might have intended that all along. It fit her canny mind, which I knew well. No one would dare to declare open rebellion, but if goaded to defend themselves and their kingdom... It all made sense.

I was the bynd to be sacrificed, removed from the playing board. It would never matter whether I conceived a son. My mother had Kral, her son. Her daughter had served her purpose.

My freedom lay in goading Rodolf to kill me as soon as possible. If he wouldn't, I'd find a way to suicide, much as it would ruin Kral's life. I know it sounds odd, that I had any concern for my younger brother. But I retained affection for him, for all of my siblings, and I felt a sort of commiseration with him, that he'd been as molded and manipulated as I.

I didn't fool myself that his life would be easy, prodded by our mother's wiles.

The guards had unlocked and opened the first set of doors, so I turned to Kral, seeing my own face in his. "I wish you well, Brother," I said, meaning it.

He bowed to me. "I wish you well, Sister. May you rejoice in your marriage and be blessed with many children—and may I meet my nephews and nieces someday."

I turned away so he wouldn't see the fresh spate of tears, though I let them fall freely when the doors locked behind me.

~ 13 ~

The ladies of the seraglio all gathered to bid me farewell. Most of them, anyway. Not Jilliya, of course, nor the ones with morning duties in the greater palace. But the rekjabrel, returned from their night's revelry, had delayed going to bed to see me off, kissing me and pressing gifts into my hands. Most of my things had already been carried out to Rodolf's caravan, but Petra had cleverly borrowed a cart the servants used to convey food and other heavy items, taking the gifts from my hands and arranging them neatly in the cart to go with us.

Her dark eyes shone with excitement, and I was glad that at least one of us faced the future with happiness in her heart.

Kaia knelt, weeping, her tears wetting my feet as she kissed them until I raised her up.

"Thank you, Princess," she said, for the umpteenth time. I'd at least been able to arrange for Kaia's retirement. My mother had, in fact, conceded to a number of my demands, eager to agree to anything, so long as I didn't make a fuss about staying married to the man who would torture and then murder me.

I'd told Inga and Helva about their gift that morning, meeting them for our last breakfast by the little lagoon. I'd called it a "bride gift," figuring that they'd only discover after I was gone that I'd made up the tradition.

Both Inga and Helva had gazed at me with blank expressions. They'd taken to dancing around me and my terrible moods, not asking questions they knew I couldn't answer. Where Harlan had been naïve and Kral had been blind, my sisters knew how things went for women. They might have been somewhat surprised to see an Imperial Princess treated no better than a rekjabrel, but I imagined they'd gotten over that quickly enough.

"What do you mean that we'll only marry if we choose it?" Inga had finally gathered her thoughts to ask.

Helva swallowed, looking down at her plate and poking at a piece of fruit. "I don't want to marry, ever."

"Then you don't have to," I reassured her, swallowing my own lump of emotion when she looked up at me, eyes swimming with tears of fearful hope. "The empress has promised, and the emperor agreed. You will both continue to be introduced to court and attend events as is traditional, and you will be presented to potential husbands, but you retain the ultimate decision. They will no doubt try to sway you, but Saira will be on guard to be sure you aren't bullied into anything you don't want to do."

Saira hadn't been shocked, exactly, when I told her of the promise I'd extracted, but she had regarded me thoughtfully and wished me well. Rather cryptically, she said that she'd do what she could to aid me in return. Knowing Saira could do nothing—a third wife who left the seraglio only with my mother's permission, or the emperor's—I thanked her as sincerely as I could, rewarded by a gentle embrace and surprising emotion in her gaze.

"What did you trade, to ensure this freedom for us?" Inga asked, her aqua eyes acute with intelligence.

"Nothing I wasn't forced to give anyway," I told her, with what I hoped looked like a wry smile. It probably came across as sad and pitiful, because her mouth trembled.

"You don't have to go," Helva said, suddenly and with ferocity. "Tell them you won't. What can they do—drag you out of here?"

"Yes," I said, decisively. "They could and would, and then I'd lose what little bargaining power I have."

Inga closed her eyes, looking pained, but nodded in reluctant agreement.

"This is my gift to you, to remember me by. If you choose to marry, choose wisely. Make sure that he is a ..." My voice broke, and I cleared my throat. "A kind man. There are some."

Inga reached over and gripped my fingers in hers, carefully avoiding my wrists. On the other side, Helva did the same. Then they joined hands with each other, completing our triangle.

"Come back to us, when you can," Inga said, her eyes intent and voice urgent. "I, at least, will stay here until you do. That's my vow to you. When you come back, I'll be waiting. And we will change all of this."

"Don't say that—" I started and she smiled at me, a ferocious baring of her teeth.

"You've bought me freedom and I won't forget it. Come back. Promise me you will."

"I can't promise that."

"Promise it," she insisted. "For I'll wait my entire life for it."

"Me, too," Helva added stoutly. "I'll wait, too. I'm never marrying so I'll be here."

"You don't know what you're saying," I told them, bewildered and yet oddly anchored by their fierce loyalty and resolve.

"We do know." Inga lifted her hand joined with Helva's, and they exchanged a look. "We're not blind to what you've suffered. Though I'd never compare my pain to yours—it's nearly killed me to stand by and be able to do *nothing* at all to help you."

Helva nodded, tears breaking and falling down her face.

"So, we're going to learn," Inga continued, voice like marble, cool and implacable. "Your mother isn't the only wily one. When you come back, we'll have all the power we can accumulate. We'll be ready."

"Ready," Helva affirmed between quiet sobs. "But promise."

"I promise I'll come back if I can," I told them, because I couldn't do otherwise. Now they stood back, hands joined, watching me from the side. Hede's women picked up the wheeled cart to carry up the stairs, and Petra adjusted the fall of my klút, then followed behind me as I passed through the doors of the seraglio for the final time.

* * * *

I made it the performance of a lifetime. Which it would be in no time at all, I had no doubt. Holding my head regally high, using all of my dancer's strength and grace, I waved to the crowds gathered to wish me farewell, determined to be remembered as an Imperial Princess, pearl of the empire.

What they don't tell you about pearls is that they're fragile jewels. Without care, without the warmth and oils of living skin, they become brittle and shatter.

When my death became known, it would be a shock, a difficult concept to reconcile with the glowing, beautiful woman I presented to them. Even Kral seemed pleased, kissing my cheek goodbye with a happy smile and what sounded like heartfelt good wishes. My mother managed to look tearful, waving to me from the emperor's side. From what I saw, anyway. I couldn't bear to look at either of them.

The guards at the great doors to the Imperial Palace lifted me in a chair to carry me the short distance to the carriage Rodolf had waiting for me. There'd been much talk of the thing—an elaborate confection of shades of ivory, trimmed with diamonds, pearls and silver spiderwebs to commemorate the joining of our three houses. Looking on it, I could only think of birdcages and Ada's story of her beloved captive bird.

Snow fell around it in thick flakes, and I spared a moment to turn my face to the white sky, savoring the way they felt, falling on my skin. A feathery brush, a spike of chill then the wetness of melt like the kiss of tears. The snowflakes seemed to manifest from nothing, emerging from the blankness and briefly spinning in their intricate, symmetrical feathers, like tiny birds, before landing on me. Then I was bundled into the carriage, happy enough for the warmth as my bare feet had gotten chilled even in those few brief moments.

I only wished I'd gotten to see the sun.

Petra rode with me in the carriage, but no one else. A relief as I didn't know how I could handle Rodolf's company without falling apart. He'd already trained me well to plead and grovel at his least command. I hated for anyone to witness it.

The interior was furnished with the softest of white fur blankets, the benches deeply padded and upholstered in ivory velvet, which also covered the walls, floor and ceiling. No windows allowed us to look out, as no commoner should be allowed to glimpse the Imperial Princess. They'd have to let me out now and again to answer the call of nature, so perhaps I'd see a bit of the outside world then. Maybe even the sun.

The carriage halted. Male voices discussing. The door opened for a guard, wearing heavy black armor, to peer in. Behind him, I caught a glimpse of the ivory sky sending out furls of snowflakes to settle over a field of fallen snow that stretched farther than my eyes had ever looked. Beyond that, a wall of real trees rose, some deep green, others mostly black and laden with snow. And beyond that, even, high mountains reared with blues and purples, the peaks I knew they must have lost in the swirl of falling snow.

The door shut, making me gasp with shock.

"Are you all right, my queen?" Petra asked. "It's so cold."

I looked at her, bemused by the mug she offered me, waving it away. If all I got were brief glimpses of outside, I'd take them clear-headed, without the muddlement of mjed. "I saw the forest. And mountains."

"The lake, too," she nodded, seeming to understand, "though it lay under the snow."

"The lake," I echoed, tasting the word. Though Ada had pronounced the landscapes painted on the walls of the seraglio clever and realistic, they didn't compare to the real outside in my eye. The real world had … incredible depth. My eyes ached from trying to see it.

"When I was brought to the Imperial Palace," Petra ventured with some hesitation, continuing when I nodded at her in encouragement, "well, it was summer. So the lake showed blue as the sky, and the mountains reflected in it, their peaks blinding white."

I tried to imagine it. Couldn't. The carriage paused, hails from the guards answered. I was ready this time, looking past the armored guard who opened the door, seeing what I could beyond him, drinking in the sight.

"There are seven guard outposts on the bridge, as I recall," Petra offered helpfully. "And one at the end. Then, if you ask, they might stop for us at the viewpoint, so you can look back on the Imperial Palace. It's a stirring sight."

I didn't care a bit about seeing the palace—well, it might be interesting, to get that perspective—but I'd take any opportunity to see outside that I could. So when the door opened the next time, I told the guard, in my best bored, imperial voice, to convey to King Rodolf that his queen requested we stop for the view of the Imperial Palace.

We finished crossing the high bridge over the lake—I was able to catch a glimpse of it stretching behind us at the final guard outpost—and the carriage wheels changed cadence as we rolled onto a solid surface. The Dasnarian Empire's famous granite roads, carefully cleared of snow for our passage. Ada had regaled us with that aspect of her journey, speaking of the workers who labored to scrape the snow away and pile it to the sides in towering walls.

After a while, we stopped. A longer stop, by the muffled sounds from outside, men calling orders and the jingling of harness. The door opened and Rodolf stood there, clad in furs, his sickeningly polite smile pinned to his fleshy mouth.

"My queen." He gestured to the waiting chair and offered a hand. "Of course you must take in the view of your imperial home."

I had no choice but to touch him—worth it to see a little more—levering myself across the gap and into the chair. Snow had fallen on the footrest, burning my bare feet, and Petra jumped into the snow with no thought for her own bare feet, wrapping mine in one of the white furs.

"Petra—your feet," I scolded her, and she gave me a look of such pleading that I immediately felt terrible for it.

"My queen, may I please see the view also?"

She had no chair, but I could hardly refuse her. "Of course. We'll find a way to warm you again."

One of the guards strode over and picked Petra up like a bundle of flowers. I expected her to stiffen or cry out in fear, but she giggled and kissed his cheek. "Alf! My hero," she sighed, and he gave her a look of great affection.

Another reason, perhaps, that Petra had been eager to leave the seraglio, if she'd found a man she liked among Rodolf's guard. It gave me a strange, queasy feeling to imagine it. Despite what I'd said to Inga and Helva, I couldn't imagine happily accepting a man's touch, even if he seemed kind. Appearances could be deceiving, and bedroom doors muffled all sorts of cries.

Rodolf led the way as two guards carried my chair. Pausing, he swept an arm at the horizon, stepping out of my way as he did. We looked down on the Imperial Palace from a rise, trees towering around us. The air smelled like … like nothing I'd ever smelled before. Bright, clean, impossibly fresh. Below, the flat basin that must be the frozen lake surrounded the gray stone Imperial Palace. It looked like the toy castles the little boys played with, and I wanted to stretch out a hand to see if I could touch it—though I knew that had to be a trick of distance.

Towers upon towers, surrounded with walls, the bridge we'd crossed a flat line over stone arches that rose out of the field of white, studded with the guardposts we'd passed through. I scanned all the rest, embedding as much of the sight as I could in my memory. The deep forest, the rise of mountains, the sounds of wind like the breathing of women in the seraglio. They were all there, somewhere under that frozen water and piles of stone, warm in their secure prison.

No wonder Ada had been so fascinated and appalled. Feeling full of a tumble of emotions, I sent her a burst of good wishes, sorry now that I'd refused to talk with her further. It wasn't her fault that I'd been a blind fool. I wiped the tears away, finding them turned to ice crystals on my fingertips.

"A moving sight, indeed," Rodolf said, noting my tears. "We'll be sure to stop for you to take in a similar vista at Castle Arynherk. Not as inspiring as the Imperial Palace, of course—nothing can match this grandeur—but it will be your home for the rest of your life." He smiled at me, wrapping his hand around my wrist just above the wedding bracelet, where the metal edges cut most deeply into my flesh when he had me strung up for his pleasure, and squeezed until I whimpered. "It's good to be taking my prize home with me, my reward for enduring your father's oppressive rule. I'm going to enjoy every moment of our marriage. As long as it lasts, that is. Say goodbye, precious Jenna."

With a last squeeze and a glitteringly cruel smile, he strode away, boots leaving holes in the pristine snow.

~ 14 ~

Do. You. Need. To. Be. Rescued.

The question components began to sound like a chant in my mind with the brisk clop of horse hooves and the rhythm of the carriage wheels on the road. After all, this would be my opportunity. I was out of the seraglio, with no locked doors between me and the outside. No series of guard outposts to check my identity. Once inside Castle Arynherk, I would be that much farther from the outside again. So, this journey was likely my one opportunity to escape.

But to where? This wasn't a time to entertain myself with pretty fantasies. I had no illusions that I wouldn't be immediately recognized. My wedding portrait had been done months before and sent throughout the empire. I'd received any number of gifts with my image replicated in embroidery or painted on cunning little boxes. Besides, I wore Rodolf's ring and wedding bracelets, locked on so I couldn't remove them myself. Even if I somehow concealed them, I'd have to show them to someone if I wanted them cut off, and then I'd be discovered.

And that was if I managed to make it to a city or town. Which I'd have to because I would be entirely helpless to feed myself. I wore a fortune in jewels, but I couldn't translate that to food and shelter without revealing my very obvious identity.

Backing up from that, even if I managed to evade the small army of Rodolf's entourage of armed guard, I'd be barefoot in deep snow, wearing only a silk klút. I supposed I could wrap myself in the furs, but I'd have to find a way to fasten them on and still I suspected that would last me only so long in the bitter temperatures. Even within the insulated carriage, the chill crept in. A servant had brought us a brazier of coals, which Petra tended with delight, as it helped a great deal to warm us.

I eyed her as she stirred the coals, letting air in to circulate and brighten them to orange-red again. Would she betray me if I tried to fashion foot coverings from the furs mounded around us? Though I had no sewing supplies. I suspected, too, that the fur would only collect snow and weigh me down. I imagined myself, slogging through the knee-deep snow, struggling to lift my feet, clutching furs around me as Rodolf's guards thundered behind.

Terrifying thought. And still not so terrifying as my husband's likely revenge for disobedience. He didn't tolerate the least resistance from me. An actual escape attempt would be beyond the pale. I supposed I could hope he'd kill me outright in that eventuality. Though that would be improbable. He'd be more inclined to keep me chained up and kill me slowly at his leisure once we reached Castle Arynherk, using the tools and implements he'd described to me in excruciating detail.

No, any escape attempt must be either completely successful or end in my immediate death. Any other outcome was unthinkable.

But how? I had no idea how to do it. And that was supposing I'd develop the spine for it.

Because I was aware, with every turn of those wheels, with every clopped-out repetition of what had become an accusation in my mind—Do. You. Need. Rescue.—that from the moment Ada had asked me that question, I'd failed utterly to have any sort of courage or strength of will. Even before that. All those years my mother taught me to obey with unquestioning alacrity, cringing away from even the threat of punishment, I'd simply gone along.

Maybe those vows Inga and Helva spoke to me had made it clear. They had a resolve I lacked. They'd promised to make things better and I thought they would. Meanwhile I sat meekly, aching from my husband's cruel attentions, going along as I'd been told to do.

I loathed myself for it.

And I had no idea how to change any of it.

* * * *

We stopped at a castle that night, and the lord greeted us with excessive excitement, beyond thrilled to host the Imperial Princess, and King Rodolf, too. I recalled the lord vaguely from my debut party, but not much more than that. I disembarked from the carriage already inside the outer walls, though I eyed them as if I could scale them as I'd once climbed the date palms, clambering over and flying away.

If I'd had more backbone, I wouldn't have let my mother forbid me from such hoydenish games after Hestar and Kral left us. Perhaps if I'd kept up those skills, climbing the walls wouldn't be so daunting. Though what would I do after? The chain of obstacles remained the same.

"Your Imperial Highness, Queen of Arynherk," the lord crooned as he bowed deeply before my carry chair after Rodolf presented me. "You honor us greatly. Our seraglio will be a poor comfort to you, I'm sure, after your imperial home, but my first wife has prepared her own apartments for you. The least thing you desire, make it known and we'll supply it."

I gazed at the bald spot on his head, pink with cold, and the feathery crown of snowflakes sticking to the sparse gray hairs around it, and nearly asked if he'd offer me asylum from my husband. Of course he wouldn't, and then Rodolf would be *angry with me*. Still, the temptation to say the words made my heart flutter with a hope I'd thought had died.

"And Your Imperial Highness Prince Harlan!" the lord exclaimed. "You honor us also. So good of you to accompany your beloved sister, the pearl of our empire, to her new home."

I managed not to reveal my shock, plastering on a serene smile and glancing over. Harlan, indeed, in full uniform and sparkling with the Konyngrr fist. He accepted the greeting, saying something in return that I couldn't process over the roar in my ears. He looked over at me and I hastily lowered my gaze, but not before I caught the grim resolve in his gray eyes.

What under Sól's all-seeing gaze could Harlan be thinking? Panic shot through me, seizing my breath and making my heart thunder.

"...all right, Your Imperial Highness?"

"Just ... chilled," I managed to say. "And weary from the journey."

That set off a flurry of activity, which fortunately diverted attention from me and my reaction to Harlan's injudicious presence. I had to send him back. My own death I could face with some measure of resolve, but not my baby brother's. They carried me into the warm interior, threatening to carry me further, but I insisted that standing would help, as I'd been sitting for hours.

It did me good, at least, to witness the effect of my commands. No one wished to displease the emperor's daughter, even to the point of ignoring Rodolf to fawn over me. My husband maintained his pleasant mien, but I caught his glittering gaze on me now and again, and I had no doubt he'd make me pay for outshining him. Even the fact that I retained my honorific of Imperial Highness over his lesser one had to rankle. As a woman, I could not elevate his rank, beyond the cachet of being married to me, but neither could the alliance lower mine.

Could I use that? I didn't know. I only knew the power of secrets, whispers, and subtle poisons. I studied Petra as she helped settle me at the table for women at the welcoming feast, ordering the servants about with borrowed precedence, ensuring that the Imperial Princess had everything she needed. Sipping the warm tea, covertly spiked with mjed as Petra arranged, I responded politely to the ladies' pretty compliments and niceties. Petra was to supply me with opos to smoke, and she'd served my mother for years—would she be able to access poisons for me? More important, was she still my mother's creature, gifted to spy upon my good behavior and report back in some way?

I wouldn't put that past my mother at all.

Harlan sat at the table with the men, naturally, in a place of precedence equal to Rodolf's. He looked so young in that company. A head shorter than most, with the promise of breadth to his shoulders but nowhere near as filled out, he seemed skinny in comparison. He had all of Helva's impetuous eagerness, and her affectionate heart, that much was clear. But gentleness and enthusiasm would get him killed. Dasnarian history was replete with "accidental" deaths of inconvenient princes. I had no doubt Rodolf could arrange for such a fate to befall my baby brother if he caused any trouble. I'd seen the man beneath the political mask—and he was a ruthless beast.

I set the mjed-spiked tea aside, instead drinking a warm brew billed as a specialty of the province by the lord's first wife. My mind worked over the options, sharper than I'd felt in days. Of course, this was also the longest I'd gone without smoking opos since my wedding night. I almost welcomed the pain and stiffness in my body, because it meant I was awake and alive.

I had no opportunity to speak with Harlan that evening, not without making too much of a point of it. And, though the castle seraglio lay behind only three sets of locked doors—and had windows that looked outside!—it was heavily guarded and presented no opportunities for escape. However, my hostess explained that at their castle, women attended meals with the men—though separated by appropriate distance—as they had no good facilities within the seraglio to feed everyone. So breakfast would be another group affair in the dining hall.

She hoped I wasn't offended by the mingling and I told her I wasn't, adding that I understood not all seraglios could be as elaborate and self-sufficient as the one at the Imperial Palace. She agreed with relief, offering me a morning tour of the castle before we dined and departed. I decided to test Petra's relative loyalty by asking her to relay a message to Harlan to join us, as I believed he'd be interested in a tour also.

I slept surprisingly well, for my first night away from the seraglio in my entire life. Though high in a tower, rather than underground, the castle seraglio smelled and sounded much like my home. Also, two nights in a row of reprieve from attending Rodolf made me languid with relief. When I did wake from dreams of wading through snow the color of blood, parts of my body falling off to be eaten by the howling hounds that tracked me, I went to the window and looked out.

They'd cunningly filled the stone arch with small panes of glass, some colored, but others clear, so I could put my eye to them and see the wintery landscape below. The overhanging clouds had cleared away, and the moon hung in a black sky, like a torque necklace of ivory trimmed in hammered silver. It looked both exactly as in paintings, and magnitudes greater. The sheer luminosity of it spilled all over the landscape, making the snow glow white and iridescent blue. The forest absorbed some of the light, but in between, several villages, little piles of orange flickerings, gathered cozily.

Everybody slept. Here in the seraglio, out there in those little towns. What sort of people lived in them? I don't know why, but it gave me a sense of peace to try to imagine their lives. It made me think of Ada, and how she'd complained about not having her husband—who she called by an affectionate nickname—in her bed and how lonely she'd been for him.

And how I so outranked my husband in every way but gender, and yet couldn't free myself of him except on these few nights.

* * * *

In the morning, I declined the offer of using the collective bath the ladies gathered in, making my refusal coldly imperious. I wouldn't have them see what Rodolf had done to my body. *Only flesh.* And yet it seemed that every vivid bruise and scabbed over wound where the lash had cut me was a testament to my lack of spine. It seemed I retained some scraps of pride and I wasn't yet willing to give them up.

Petra knew, of course, as had the women of my home seraglio, but they had been family. So Petra brought me a basin of water and helped me sponge bathe, rubbing in the numbing cream painstakingly scented with jasmine to match my usual perfume. I donned yet another concealing klút, augmented with scarves and a pearl-embroidered overcloak, using the excuse that I wasn't accustomed to the cold outside the imperial seraglio.

My hostess—chagrined and wishing to make up for the faults she perceived in her own home—had servants pacing us with warming beverages on the tour of the castle. Harlan joined us, offering his arm to me and making charming conversation with our hostess.

The castle provided startling delights to my untutored eye. The back side of the structure held a room with large windows, filled with clear glass in larger diamonds, and overlooking a long garden with an unfrozen pond, all within the high outer walls. Birds flew in to land upon it, inscribing ripples across its dark surface.

"It's fed by natural hot springs below," our hostess explained with some pride, "so many birds overwinter here, taking advantage. We put out seed to help them along, as well."

I marveled at them, so many birds I'd never seen, even in paintings and tapestries. "Have you elephants?" I asked.

One of the secondary wives tittered before she hastily suppressed it, and my hostess regarded me with wide, astonished eyes. "Why… no, Your Imperial Highness. There are none in all of the Dasnarian Empire. You'd have to travel to Halabahna to see those."

Oh. My mother's training kept me from showing embarrassment at my ignorance, but I fought a well of disappointment in my heart. A silly thing to be sorry about given my other, much greater concerns. Just then the ivory mist shifted and the light brightened.

"Ah," my hostess enthused, happy to have something to offer in lieu of elephants, I supposed. "The sun is burning through. You'll have a fine day for travel."

I blinked my eyes against the sun's fire, never having guessed at its power. It actually hurt to look at, much as I tried. It made my eyes burn as if I'd touched actual fire, tears leaking from the corners.

"Are you all right, Jenna?" Harlan asked, sounding boyishly anxious.

"Ask our hostess to fetch me a cool cloth, please."

He did, and as soon as she did, Petra going to assist, I said, "I've never seen it before, you know."

"Never seen what? You shouldn't stare at the sun so—you'll damage your eyes."

"Truly?" I whispered. "That's how it feels. So amazing. It's brighter than I could have imagined."

"You've never seen the sun," Harlan said slowly, as if having a difficult time assimilating the information.

It made me laugh. "Well, when would I have?"

"I don't know," he replied, sounding annoyed, though maybe not with me. "I never gave it any thought. I never gave any thought to far too many things."

Petra returned with the cloth floating in a bowl of herbs, our hostess fluttering anxiously in her wake. Harlan led me to a chair, knelt at my side and held the bowl he took from Petra. "Give Her Imperial Highness some room," he ordered. "She needs a moment of quiet."

They backed off to the other side of the room, leaving me bemused at how easily Harlan created a moment for us to talk. I could do this, too, leverage my rank while I had the ability to do so. I wrung out the cloth and dabbed at my face, presenting the image of a woman overcome by a dizzy spell.

"Why are you here?" I asked into the scented cloth. The spiciness cleared my senses of emotional murk, and now my mind raced ahead. "Never mind. You must go back."

"I'm not leaving you with *him*," Harlan replied, just as quietly, granite in his voice.

I glanced at him, seeing the man he might become someday. But not today. He was a boy confronting powers he could never fight. "I'm married to him. Nothing can change that."

"Maybe that's so, but you can escape to where he'll never find you."

He looked so earnest, his gray eyes so clear and uncluttered by the fear that dragged at me. Such shining and foolish naivete. "To where?" I asked.

He frowned a little. "I haven't worked out the details, but I will."

"No you won't." I shook my head. "Because there is no place he won't find me. Even if there were, I have no way to travel. I'm barefoot and helpless, and imperial law stands against me. Go home, Harlan, I beg you."

"I won't." The stubborn set of his jaw reminded me of Helva, bringing fresh tears to my eyes. "I'm not just meekly giving up without even trying. You're a Konyngrr, too. Why won't you at least fight your fate?"

That struck me through the heart, because I hadn't fought. Thought I couldn't.

"What's this?" Rodolf boomed, entering the room with the castle lord. "My wife is unwell? My pearl, say it isn't so."

I fixed a smile into place and stood to greet him, averting my eyes in a show of obedience. "It isn't so. A momentary spell. I'm fine."

But I wasn't. Because I began to hope for real escape, and the possibility hurt more than I could have ever thought.

~ 15 ~

We traveled all that day, stopping only rarely, mostly at imperial guard stations hastily cleaned so the Imperial Princess could use facilities primarily intended for men. Women simply didn't travel, one commander told me, fascinating me with his lack of polished manners. He apologized for the rudimentary amenities and reiterated several times what an honor I did them by gracing their remote outpost with my royal presence.

If Rodolf's entourage hadn't outnumbered those loyal guards by five to one, I might have considered asking them to fight for me. From the grizzled commander to the bright-eyed youths, younger even than Harlan, they regarded me with such dazzled admiration I thought they'd do anything for me.

Even die, which was what would happen. Though their outpost made a fine fortress, even if they could sequester me inside and hold off Rodolf, my father would muster enough of an army to break through. Those that survived any such battle would be dealt with as traitors. I'd heard enough gruesome stories that I couldn't wish that on anyone at all.

Except perhaps Rodolf.

I amused myself with spinning that concept on the hours of riding in the confines of the carriage. It seemed even dimmer for the bright sun that greeted me every time we stopped. Every time I'd stare at it as long as I could, the glory of it leaving its impressions inside my eyes for me to marvel at behind my lids. Perhaps the custom of women averting their eyes came from protecting them against the sun's blistering presence in the sky. But it burned male eyes, too, I'd learned, so perhaps not.

Petra dozed, and so I contemplated how I might make Rodolf seem the traitor in my father's eyes. The emperor would not bestir himself on my behalf for being used roughly. What a man did with his wife sexually was his business, I understood that well. That is the way of things. I belonged to Rodolf, his to feed, clothe, and protect—and in return he received the use of my body.

But I knew Rodolf plotted with the Elskadyrs to take the throne. Difficult to guess what my mother's deep laid plan might be, though surely it wouldn't be exactly what Rodolf believed. If I could somehow spur him to act against the emperor's interests, even unwittingly...

I couldn't yet think of a way, but it seemed with time the opportunity might arise. Perhaps I could cozen him into enjoying me enough not to kill me too soon. If I could get with that heir he wanted, that would help immensely. A distant part of me stood aside, observing that I'd found plenty of spine as I healed—and having had two glorious nights without Rodolf's brutally humbling attentions. I plotted happily enough without the nightly reminder of how thoroughly he owned me.

Still, if I came up with a good enough plan, I might be able to persuade Harlan to give up his impossible dream of somehow liberating me. I needed him to go home and the only way he'd do that was if he trusted that I'd survive on my own.

Two things happened later that afternoon unfortunately; Rodolf seemed to notice my renewed spirits, and the clouds gathered, bringing snowfall with them. This far between major cities, snow accumulated on the road, slowing the wheeled vehicles. I listened to the shouts and orders, Rodolf sending men ahead to clear the way, but they seemed to be able to work only so fast, and not nearly enough to keep us at the needed pace to reach the castle that was our next destination.

We would have to stay at an inn, Rodolf informed me. He climbed into the carriage, brusquely ordering Petra out into the snow, and still overwhelming the space with his bulk. "We have to take measures, my pearl," he said, in that kind voice that boded terrible things, "in order to protect you as befitting your rank and station. Thus you'll sleep in my room with me."

I nodded, not trusting my voice, all of my thoughts scattering before the shrieking winds of terror.

"And it's best if you're not recognized," he continued. "Wrists behind your back, my darling."

I obeyed without hesitation, having learned that one early, and at pain of the whip. He fastened my wedding bracelets together, then offered me a large silver ball. I knew this one, too, and obediently opened my mouth to hold it on my tongue while he fastened one of my scarves over it to hold it in place. "Just in case you're tempted to speak to anyone," he whispered in my ear. "I feel I've been neglecting you and you have gotten a rebellious gleam in your eye. I wouldn't want you to contemplate anything foolish."

He covered me with a heavy cloak, plain and unadorned. Then took a knife and cut my klút so my breasts were bared beneath. "A bit of insurance," he explained, kneading them painfully. "If you struggle at all, the cloak will fall open and show the imperial tits to all the world. You don't want that, do you?"

I shook my head, humiliated to be racked with shuddering fear. I'd promise him anything at that moment. An entire night in his rooms. Tears spilled out of me at the prospect.

"Weep if you must. You know I love that evidence of my effect on you. Maybe I should show them all how the emperor's daughter grovels for me. One day—not far in the future—it will be your father, begging for my mercy. Maybe I'll let you watch as you've brought me closer to the end game. But be silent, or I won't be so kind as I have been."

I was silent. I walked barefoot through the snow under the shroud of my cloak, the hood tied over my face so I had to be led, into the inn and up the stairs to the grandest room, the innkeeper promised. Though not fit for a noble lady, he apologized profusely.

Rodolf dismissed him, saying it would be fine. In a parody of caring, he let me warm my feet before he started on me. After all, he said, it wouldn't do for me to lose any toes, as frostburn was so unsightly. Certain marks and bruises served to enhance my beauty, but he would never see his pearl disfigured. He also waited until the servants—not Petra; I had no idea where she'd gotten to—brought food and wine, before he locked the door and unwrapped me.

I never did eat, as he never removed the gag. No sense inspiring foolish heroics in anyone, Rodolf explained, in that very practical tone. My little brother, for example, seemed unduly concerned that I wasn't happy. Apparently I needed some reminders about discipline and presenting the proper front, as an imperial princess should.

That night of lessons, conducted in whispers and whimpers, was the worst of all.

* * * *

Rodolf left me in the morning to breakfast with the men, sending Petra to tend me. With the foresight of the seraglio, she arranged for plenty of extra water to sluice the mostly dried blood away. She hid me behind a screen for the inn servants to bring in my trunk of travel clothes, and then the additional water, though she dumped the soiled water out the window, and burned the bloodstained clothes and cloths.

She also brought in my pipe and plied me with opos and mjed, both, and I clung to the numbing succor without another thought for keeping my mind clear. That obviously only led to pain. With the help of opos, I could present a dreamy smile for Harlan.

And it helped to feel the claws of terror ease. As Petra carefully wrapped me in a swathing klút, I watched her. "Where did you spend last night?" I asked.

She started, and I realized I hadn't yet spoken to her. "His Highness King Rodolf said you had no need of me. I apologize, Your Imperial Highness."

"Not that. I knew that. Where did you sleep?"

She averted her gaze, high pink on her cheeks. "With Alf, in Rodolf's guard. He paid for a room for us."

"Ah." I mulled that over, wondering if she'd gone cheerfully or if that had been the price of a bed. One that I should have bought for her, had I been... *Don't think about it.* Still. "I don't want you paying your passage with your body," I said. "Take some pearls."

She started to laugh and smothered in, controlling herself. "You are kind and generous, Your Imperial Highness, but—I know the outside world is new to you and thus mean no criticism in any way—but women cannot handle payment."

Of course. I did know that, somewhere in the back of my mind. Rodolf should see to Petra, but I couldn't see myself asking him for that. Though I should. She was my responsibility. If I asked, however... I began to shake and took a deep toke from the pipe to steady myself.

"It's all right, Your Imperial Highness," Petra said, tears leaking from her eyes. She took the pipe and refilled it generously, giving it back to me. "I like Alf. Don't worry for me."

"But you weep," I pointed out, feeling dreamier.

"For you," she replied softly. "My tears are for you." She bit her lip and dashed them away, huddling in anticipation of reprimand. My mother would likely have had her punished for daring to pity a noble. Such was my extremity that I felt only gratitude in that moment.

"Then he's not ... cruel to you?" I asked.

Her eyes flew to mine, wide and earnest. "Oh no. Most men are *not* like, ah..."

"My esteemed husband," I finished for her on a long sigh. But hearing that helped in a way. Though I'd already known it. Ada speaking of her

Freddy with obvious affection. The rekjabrel who came to the seraglio because they'd fallen in love with certain men in the Imperial Palace and tended to those men, and them only.

Shouts from below, the sounds of horses and carriage wheels. "Can you be ready to go, Your Imperial Highness?" Petra asked, sounding not at all sure. "I can say you need more time."

No. I wanted to leave that horrible room. Not that it was the place's fault, but I wanted to be in the open air again. Maybe seeing the sun would burn some of the long night away. "I'm ready. Is the sun shining?" It didn't look like it from where I stood, and Rodolf had forbidden me from going near the windows.

"No, Your Imperial Highness." Petra brought the cloak, warm from the fire, and gently wrapped me in it, pulling the cowl deeply around my face, but not tying it. "Keep your head bowed and no one will guess it isn't tied," she whispered, as if we could be overheard. Then more loudly, "It's cloudy and snowing."

"Perhaps it will clear." I let her lead me out the door and down the steps.

"Perhaps so, my lady," she replied. But I could tell she didn't think so.

* * * *

I slept the day away in a dreamy fog. Petra kept the brazier hot, and the opos and mjed at hand. An advantage of not sleeping all night was that I napped for long and depthless stretches, my dreams bloody and full of pain, but the opos muted them. Like the blank ivory sky and the endless snowfall, muffling everything.

We still traveled slowly, though a bit faster than we had when it began to snow. Rodolf had men working for miles in advance of our entourage, clearing the road, so Petra said during one of my short waking spells. If I had not been born in midwinter, we would not have encountered such difficulties, Rodolf had told me the night before. One of my many flaws.

When we stopped at a guard outpost to use the facilities, my body had stiffened so that I stumbled stepping out of the carry chair. Several guards leapt forward to steady me, Harlan first among them. He gave me a long look, but said nothing, only offered me his arm to lean on while I shuffled to yet another hastily cleaned facility.

"I'm arranging to ride with you," he murmured to me, when I emerged and Petra took her turn. Women first, and then the men would have their opportunity. "Can your girl be trusted?"

I shook my head. Too much risk, despite Petra's sympathy. "Mother gave her to me." He nodded in crisp understanding, and I gathered my blurred wits. "But Harlan, don't. You must go."

He patted my hand, smiling at Petra as she emerged. "Let's get you back in the carriage, Sister."

He flanked the carry chair, telling one of the men to take care of his horse. "I don't know how you all stand this cold," he complained. "I'm riding in the carriage a while."

The men hooted and hollered, calling him worse than a female. He bore it with good grace, then made a mention of life at the Imperial Palace that cut off the derision, the men abruptly reminded of Harlan's rank as an Imperial Prince, no matter his age or apparent weakness.

He helped me into the carriage, bundling the fur blankets around me with care. Studying the pipe and chest of opos leaves, he made a face, but set them carefully aside, to make room for Petra. She seemed greatly perplexed, but naturally wouldn't question him. When she moved to prepare my pipe, however, he stopped her. "Leave off that for now. The smoke bothers my eyes."

Not like him, to be so preemptory, little as I knew him in truth. Despite his protestations of being cold, he refused the furs Petra offered him, and folded his arms, settling back and appearing to doze. I did, too, enough of the opos still in me to make me drowsy. I curled up on the seat and slept.

A while later, the carriage halted, and I blinked against the heaviness of my eyelids, sitting up. The door opened and Alf stood there, giving Petra a cocky grin. "Bring a blanket and come ride with me, little dove. If Her Imperial Highness permits, of course."

Petra looked to me with hope bright in her eyes, and I waved her on. Harlan seemed to be asleep, though I noted Alf asked only my permission. My brother played a dangerous game and the price would come out of my skin. We started up again and I reached for my pipe.

Harlan's eyes snapped open, fully alert. "Leave it," he said quietly. "I need your mind sharp."

~ 16 ~

I confess I nearly hurled the thing at him. Who cared what *he* needed? I needed the opos to drown out the pain, and the crawling terror of what might next happen. Especially if Rodolf suspected, which he would. Oh, he would.

"You have to not talk to me," I explained, trying to be clear and calm. It had sounded so easy to promise when Rodolf drilled the words into me.

Harlan only snorted, leaning forward and bracing his forearms on his knees. "I know he has you terrorized, but I'm an Imperial Prince and I outrank Rodolf. If I want to ride with my beloved sister, I will."

Tears spilled out in a helpless wave, and I didn't even try to stop them. "It's not you he'll punish."

Harlan went very still, but fury rose behind his solemn gray eyes. "What does he do to you?" he asked quietly, with an intensity beyond his years.

I laughed a little, trying to muffle the hysterical edge, but he clearly caught it. "There are things you don't discuss with your baby brother," I managed.

"I'm not a child, Jenna."

"Nor are you a man," I retorted.

Rather than becoming annoyed, he tapped his fingers together, studying his hands. "I'm aware of that. If I could add to my years at this moment, immediately wish onto myself the muscle and fighting ability I might gain in the years ahead, I'd sacrifice anything for that. You should know that."

Stricken I pressed my lips together and nodded. "That was wrong of me. I didn't mean to insult you."

"You didn't." He cracked a smile. "I'm keenly aware of my shortcomings in my ability to extract you from this situation, but I'm going to do it anyway. We're going to do it, together."

"But why would you?" It came out as a plea.

"Because it's the right thing to do. I won't stand by and let this happen to you. I'm getting you away from him, whatever it takes."

I was shaking my head, a low moan escaping me before I stoppered it. "Don't speak those words. It's impossible."

"Nothing is impossible," he replied with all that optimistic earnestness he shared with Helva.

"It *is*." We were conducting the conversation in the lowest of voices, but my skin still twitched with the expectation that Rodolf would wrench open the door and discover us. "I'm not so lacking in Konyngrr spine that I haven't thought about it. But I have no shoes, no warm clothes. I'm instantly recognizable and I have nowhere to go. And if I don't get away completely—" I had to pause to swallow down the sick, remembering Rodolf's promises, the dreams of the howling dogs eating the pieces of my body as they fell from me while I struggled through the snow. "I would be dead. Worse than dead—and so would you."

Harlan smiled, the cockiness of youth and grim resolve of character in it. "Then I'll make sure we get away completely. Can you trust me to do that?"

I didn't know. Fear riddled and weakened me, making me feel stooped and aged as Old Mara. But I didn't want to be that bird who stayed in her cage, afraid to fly out the open window.

"Yes," I said. *Do you need to be rescued?* "Yes."

"Good." Harlan nodded at me. "I know this takes a lot of courage. You are amazing."

"I'm not brave," I told him.

"But you are, because he hasn't broken you. Leave it to me. Be ready to go when I say. The hardest part—no mjed or opos, or even gryth. Can you do that?"

I firmed my mouth and nodded. I would, no matter what.

"How much pain are you in without it?" He asked carefully.

"Some."

"Answer me like a dancer. How would your gauge your strength and stamina? Be honest."

"I have no broken bones, but I'm weakened. I doubt I can endure much."

"All right." He closed his eyes briefly, swallowing something down. "If we maintain the present pace, we'll stop at Castle Fjaltyndar where we meant to stop last night. Pray it keeps snowing like this. But it's looking inevitable at this point. Plead illness or weariness and ask to go straight to the seraglio. Act weak enough that I must carry you there."

"You can't carry me into the seraglio—you won't be allowed. Not without grave insult to our hosts."

Harlan gave me a grim smile. "I'm an Imperial Prince. They should be worried about insulting me. Now, once there, feign sleep if you must, but stay alert. Wear your darkest klút. Have you hair tied up so it won't show. Be ready."

Part of me had always realized men didn't enter by custom, not because they couldn't if they decided to. But I didn't understand how he planned to get me out of the seraglio again and said so.

"I'll take care of the guards outside. Don't worry about that."

"And the inside guards?"

He frowned. "Do you think one this small will have guards inside, too?"

"Probably," I said. "The last one did."

He muttered a curse. "I'll think of something."

"No," I said, surprising myself now. "I can make them sleep." Sól knew I had enough gryth to make a dozen women sleep soundly.

Harlan studied me. "I've heard rumors. About … the empress and certain herbs. No offense intended toward your mother, who I assume you hold dear."

I laughed a little, for his sweetness and his delicacy. "Poison, I think, is the word you're looking for. And I do *not* hold her dear. She—" I had to break off there, robbed of breath, unexpected black and bilious fury rising up to choke me.

Face creased, Harlan reached out a hand to me, then let it fall, clearly unsure what to do for me. "Jenna?" he asked, tentative. Making me wonder what he saw in my face.

"Don't worry. I'll make sure they sleep and I'll be ready. As for a place to go—Princessa Adaladja of Robsyn offered to help me."

"Did she now?" Harlan mulled that over, then shook his head. "Robsyn is too deep into the empire, too far from the coasts if you're discovered."

"I wouldn't want to bring that on her, regardless." Speaking of which, "I want you to promise me something."

He raised his brows, saying nothing.

"If we're caught, you abandon me and go straight back to the Imperial Palace. Don't let them kill you."

"Our father will hardly welcome me back with open arms in that eventuality," Harlan pointed out.

"But he won't let you be killed."

"I'm his seventh son, far down on the list of spare heirs. There's nothing for me there. I'm not going back. I'm going with you."

I nearly gasped. "You can't! To where?"

"I have an idea of where, and did you think I'd abandon you somewhere without protection, without a way to pay for even your food?"

"I don't know!" Somehow when he asked me to trust him, I'd imagined him finding another seraglio for me, one I could hide in for the rest of my life. What would the rest of my life look like? I couldn't even imagine. And it was too huge to contemplate. All that mattered now was getting away. "But you can't give up your birthright, your title, your entire life for me."

He gave me a slight smile. "I'm looking at it as trading for something better. The empire is big, but the world is bigger. You said you wanted to see an elephant, didn't you? Sounds like a fine goal to me."

* * * *

Harlan continued to ride in the carriage even after Petra returned, cheeks pink with snow chill and lips full from kissing. She offered me my pipe, perplexed when I refused, more so when I asked to have my tea plain, without gryth or mjed. For that I subtly blamed Harlan, sliding a glance at him to remind her how the men disapproved of women indulging in the liquor. She nodded knowingly and curled up for her own nap.

Harlan and I chatted amiably, speaking of our siblings. He filled me in on our brothers' doings, who was good at what field of study or style of fighting. The only exception was Hestar, whom he touched on only briefly. He didn't exactly make his dislike clear, but I understood from what he didn't say how Hestar both held himself apart and made his younger brothers' lives more difficult.

Harlan asked about some of the ladies in the seraglio, including Old Mara. "She told the best stories," he commented, wistfulness in his voice. "I miss visiting her."

"I'm surprised you remember her."

He regarded me with an odd expression. "I remember a lot about my childhood in the seraglio. It seems like a paradise in my mind—all warmth and lush flowers, waterfalls and lagoons. I was broken hearted to be summarily expelled from it. It seemed terribly unfair that you and Inga—and especially Helva—got to stay and I didn't."

I glanced at the apparently sleeping Petra. Unfortunate that she was likely my mother's tool. "We missed you, too. Especially Helva." I didn't say that we found it terribly unfair we didn't get to leave. By the way

Harlan's eyes rested on me, the thoughts turning behind them, I suspected he'd realized that.

And, like me, he'd begun to see that our childhood paradise wasn't what we'd believed it to be at all.

* * * *

I didn't have to pretend much to appear unwell when we reached Castle Fjaltyndar. Without opos or mjed, or even the milder sedative of gryth to cushion me, every jolt of the carriage had become an agony. The world had gone gray and I felt faint. We stopped and Harlan gathered me up, carrying me out of the carriage—not an easy task, maneuvering us out the narrow door, but holding me easily.

"My sister is unwell," he informed Rodolf and the lord who greeted us, wasting no time. I buried my face in Harlan's chest, so I wouldn't glimpse my husband's expression and lose my nerve. "Lead me to the seraglio," Harlan demanded, every bit as arrogant as Hestar could ever be.

He strode along and I fuzzed out for a while. I heard some protests that he couldn't enter, and him saying to hide the ladies away or blindfold him or whatever they needed to do, but unless someone else wanted to carry me, he was going in. He was an Imperial Prince and no one could gainsay him.

They must have let him, because next thing I knew, Harlan was tenderly laying me on a divan of pillows so soft my body melted into them. He pressed something into my hand, kissing my cheek as he did. "Stimulants. Take them. Can you make it?"

"Yes." I levered my eyes open, folding the herbs into my palm. "After all, I slept the day away."

He laughed. "They're having someone tend you, but don't sleep. No sedatives."

"I know."

He rose, covering his eyes with his big hands—they reminded me of a puppy we'd had with too-large paws that forecast his eventual size, exiling him, too, from the seraglio. I giggled, giddy for no reason. Except maybe because, no matter what happened tonight, Rodolf would never touch me again. If it looked like we'd be captured, I'd kill myself. I no longer had any doubt of my ability to do that.

Death, at least, would be painless.

* * * *

This seraglio was smaller even than the previous one. Really a series of rooms little larger than my apartments had been. And with windows. Glassed in, from what I could see, but only a thin width to the outside.

The healing woman brought me hot water when I asked, saying I had my own special herbs from the Imperial Palace. Secret ones only for Imperial Princesses, I said, so I must brew them in private. I didn't want to risk that she might recognize them by sight or scent as stimulants.

I brewed it strong and drank it fast, amazed by the potency that seized my nerves and sent my heart pounding. At least I had no fear of sleeping. I also allowed only Petra to tend to me, letting her change my bandages and rub the muscle-coolant the healer gave her into my aching body.

Even if I could trust her, however, what kind of life would she have outside of the empire? No one in their right mind would leave the pinnacle of civilization for the barbaric lands beyond the emperor's enforced order, peace, and prosperity.

Fortunately, I'd long since lost my right mind. I didn't know why Harlan had, but I'd seize the opportunity he gave me. Maybe we would make it. There was something I could picture for my life after—doing everything I could to ease Harlan's way. I'd spend the rest of my life repaying him.

My nerves ready to snap like delicate silk thread, I lay there, listening to the soft conversation of the ladies who'd remained in the seraglio, then the return of the few who'd dined with the esteemed visitors. At that point, I roused myself, drifting out to sit with the ladies, to make acquaintance and to apologize. My delicate constitution and the horrors of travel. How lovely to rest in the security of their seraglio. Oh, no—it wasn't small or plain at all—so cozy and delightful.

Then, my heart hammering as I turned out not to be very good at this sort of subterfuge, I asked Petra to bring out the other pot of tea I had brewing. The sedative gryth tea, also made extra strong—as I'd asked her to make it—and more than half mjed. They all should share it with me, as a gesture of my appreciation.

Petra gave me a few sidelong glances, but poured as I instructed. She would not defy me directly. Even this far from the Imperial Palace, I could have a defiant servant killed with a few words. And the ladies, of course, didn't dare refuse the gift. Not wishing to offer insult, they all drank—some working hard not to gag or make faces—even the guards, when I coaxed them prettily as deserving a reward for guarding us all so diligently.

Petra, I thought, only pretended to drink. Something that I fretted over. But I hadn't been able to think of a way to circumvent her. If only I could trust her to collude with me. I feigned sleep, and I thought she did, too, lying on a servant's pile of blankets on the floor next to me. If Harlan came, he'd trip over her, and wake her.

Then—nearly a miracle—Petra answered a summons to attend Alf. Handy that she would be occupied, though I wondered if Harlan had somehow encouraged the liaison. Perhaps she'd been meeting Alf every night and I'd been too doped up to realize.

Petra would be on her own when I'd fled. I could only hope she would be cared for. My mother's spy or not, Petra had been kind to me, tending me carefully.

Occupying myself with details, my mind racing while the others slept deeply, I tried to work out what Harlan's plan might be. How could he possibly extract me from the seraglio? He'd tricked his way in, certainly, getting the feel for the layout, I felt sure, despite his ostentatiously covered eyes.

It would have to be the windows. Though how he'd open them without alerting the outside guard I didn't know. Then, as the hours passed, I began to fret that Harlan wouldn't come. Or that Petra would return before he did.

Or that he'd been discovered. Soon I'd hear shouts and angry voices. Even an Imperial Prince would pay a price for trying to steal into the seraglio.

A movement caught my ears. Not a snuffle-snort of sleep, but … something. Moving as silently as I could, I sat up.

And there was Harlan on the floor, down on hands and knees and gesturing for me to do the same.

Though my body protested, I slid quietly off the bed, mimicking him, promising my abused flesh that if it would just keep going it would never suffer again. Never would I chafe at a life of leisure and luxury. I followed behind Harlan, crawling to the door, my heart loud in my ears. Klúts aren't made for crawling, but I did my best. It helped that he didn't hurry, keeping slow and stealthy.

As he'd told me, I'd braided my hair and removed all my jewelry— customary for bed, regardless—except my gloves, the wedding bracelets and ring, of course. The gloves helped, but to keep the chains from jingling, I'd wrapped my hands in extra scarves. We made it to the inner door, Harlan easing it open, then crawling through. Placing my trust in him, I followed. No guards there, though I didn't know if there hadn't been any or if Harlan had somehow disposed of them. Only two locked doors in this place, and the lights beyond the outer one blazed into my eyes after the dark of the nighttime seraglio when Harlan eased open that door. Signaled me to wait. He rose and went out, then came back and gestured me to stand and come with him.

My hand enfolded in his big one, I slipped out the door into the hall, surprised to find the two male guards sleeping, one snoring mightily. Harlan produced a key and locked the door. Smiling at me, he led me down the hall where it grew dimmer, then down a narrow, unadorned staircase, such as servants might use.

We emerged into a quiet kitchen, lit only by a low-burning fire, slipping through it quickly, then down into a musty-smelling cellar. Harlan had me wait while he shifted a few barrels, then sent me up a wide, shallow set of stairs to crouch under a wooden roof. He crawled in behind me, replacing the barrels behind us, plunging us into darkness.

The roof above me creaked, and I realized he was levering it open. He did just enough to peek out, then let it fall. He counted under his breath, then lifted again. Looked briefly. Closed and counted. Looked again.

He put his mouth to my ear. "When I say go, run as fast as you can. Don't look around. Don't worry about your feet. It will be ice and snow over stone. Your bare toes will give you decent footing. Across the yard you'll see an open door with a torch on either side. Run straight for that, turn left and crouch down. Don't move. Count to sixty and I'll be behind you."

"Yes," I replied, not bothering to tell him I had no idea how much sixty was. I'd simply wait. I'd wait there until Harlan came for me or someone else found me. I had no choice.

Harlan eased the roof open, watching, closed it and counted. I tried to memorize how long that was. "Ready..." He eased the roof open. Looked. Pushed it wider for me to slide out. "Go!"

~ 17 ~

My klút caught, ripping, and I yanked it, the hiss of silk whispering loud in the nighttime courtyard.

Then I ran.

Dark all around. Punctuated by torches. Looming walls and shadows. The pair of torches dead ahead, flanking a black doorway.

Ice and slush under my feet, mixed in with gritty dirt.

I ran with all my might, with all my dancer's speed and agility. The performance of a lifetime.

My heart ran as fast as my feet, a panicked cadence that spurred me on. Even if my heart burst, I'd die quickly. A far better death.

Far better than the grasping hands I expected to seize me at any moment.

And I was between torches, inside the doors. Turn left. Piles of scratchy plant material, packed tight, making a little wall. I crouched there, tucked back in my prickly cubby. Something cut into my foot, but I didn't care. I stayed as still as I could, willing my heart to quiet so I could hear.

Horses, the smell stronger than the sound, but all around in this warm place. As instructed, I hadn't looked around as I ran, only straight ahead, but my peripheral vision is keen and practiced. I'd run across the outer courtyard and into the stables.

I think none of the patrolling guards saw me. No alarm had gone up.

But no Harlan, either.

Had it been a count of sixty? I'd forgotten how long that should feel like. It seemed like ages, regardless, that I crouched there. What would I do if Harlan never came? I'd escaped from the seraglio—disobedience of such a scale that I'd be punished even by the kindest of husbands. Here, where

I'd shame both my husband and my hosts... I couldn't imagine. They'd have to make an example of me.

If Harlan didn't come, what would I do?

It crystallized for me then—in that moment that I had no ability to even measure by a count of heartbeats, that has expanded in my mind so large that it's edged out many other memories of that night—how utterly helpless I was to save myself.

Without Harlan's help, I could never have escaped. My rank, my beauty, my fortune—everything I'd thought valuable about myself meant absolutely nothing, because I depended on others for everything. Even to stay alive.

No more. I might be the flower carefully raised and cut from her garden, but I refused to wither and die. I would find a way to feed myself. To survive.

And then Harlan was there.

Putting his lips against my ear, he spoke quietly. "Well done. We're clear so far. Behind you are cloaks and packs. Feel them? The sound of the horses will cover us somewhat, but be quiet."

I rummaged around, wondering if all that time had been truly only his count of sixty. Perhaps so, as he didn't say otherwise. An eternity of time for me, during which I'd become someone else.

Finding the bundles of cloth, I handed them to him. He shook out one and draped it over me, then handed me something furry.

"Boots," he explained quietly. "For your feet," he added, as I was clearly an addle-headed idiot incapable of figuring that out.

They weren't hard to put on, just odd feeling. My feet felt smothered and cramped, the stiffness pinching a little. Nothing like the pain Rodolf had caused me, however, so it was easy to ignore.

Harlan took my hand. "This way."

I walked behind him, trying to keep my balance, feeling oddly as I had the night of my bethrothal with my long, jeweled toenails. The boots had soft fur on the inside, but they were awkward and slid around on my feet in odd places, grabbing in others. I also had no feeling for the ground on the other side of the thick bottoms, and the toes kept hanging up on things.

Fortunately he went slowly, pausing often to listen and watch for movement. We threaded through shadowed corridors of high posts and walls, broken by lower ones. Once a horse thrust its head at me, and I flinched, startled, but didn't make a sound. I'd learned that lesson well enough.

We reached a far end, and Harlan led me into a large boxy room for horses, with two inside. "I put them together," he said to me, quietly, "but didn't saddle them yet in case a groom noticed. It will only take a moment."

He lifted a blanket onto the patient horse, which looked so big from where I stood, then a saddle. He added a bridle, and our packs, then gestured to me. "Climb on. The back door is right here and we can ride them out."

My heart broke a little, the shame rising at my complete uselessness. "Harlan—I can't ride a horse. This is the closest I've ever been to one."

He scrubbed a hand over his face. "I'm an idiot. We'll take one horse and lead the other. You can ride behind me."

I nodded, unwilling to be even more of a problem, but having no idea how I'd bear putting the horse against my sore nether regions. I would simply do it. I'd have to. Harlan quickly saddled the second horse, attaching a long lead to it, then swung into the saddle, holding a hand down to me. "Put your foot onto mine and I'll pull you up. You have strong legs—you can do it."

I could. And did. But, though I braced myself for it, the shock of contact against my tormented woman's parts sent such a blaze of agony through me that blackness rose up, my gorge rising. I held onto Harlan and stayed upright through some force of will I dredged up. It might hurt, but Rodolf would never touch me again.

I might die, but Rodolf would never touch me again.

Rodolf would never touch me again.

* * * *

I don't remember much else of that night. Perhaps it's best that those agonizing hours are lost.

Somehow we rode out of Castle Fjaltyndar—through some unguarded back gate, it must have been. There was dark forest, lots of snow, lots of cold. My bare legs under the cloak grew numb with chill, where my klút was hiked up to allow me to sit astride, but at least my feet were warm. I locked my hands around Harlan's waist and tried not to think about how much I hurt.

I didn't exactly sleep—the stimulants Harlan had me drink were amazingly strong—but I fell into some kind of trance. Maybe I'd finally reached the point where I simply couldn't handle any more, and my mind stopped working.

* * * *

Sometime after it stopped being night, but settled into a gray-white version of daylight, we stopped at some cabin. It looked very small, but the prospect of not being on the horse filled me with delirious gratitude. Harlan circled around it, coming up behind where there stood a small shed. Some snow sifted inside, but nothing like the hip-deep stuff he sank into when he slid off our mount.

He held up hands to me and I remember staring at him, unsure what to do. "Jump down," he urged. "I'll catch you."

I shook my head, aware of what he'd see if I did. The shame too much to bear. For all I'd wanted off that horse more than anything—or so I'd thought—I didn't want my baby brother to witness my feminine humiliation.

"Turn your back," I said.

He glared at me, exasperated—and also clearly exhausted. "I'm too tired for this. You're cold as it is. Jump down and I'll carry you inside. We need to get a fire started. Every moment you stall out of whatever misplaced missishness is driving you, is another moment we could be resting and getting warm before we have to go again."

The whip of impatience in his voice found my well-trained senses, and I obeyed. He caught me, carried me inside the cold and dark interior, then set me on my feet. I wobbled, and my legs gave way. Fortunately I managed it with some grace, making it look as if I folded myself onto a warm and furry rug.

Harlan fumbled in the dark, then a flicker of flame became a blaze, illuminating a pile of logs inside a stone fireplace. "Keep feeding it," Harlan instructed, pointing at the logs in a basket nearby. "I'll take care of the horses and be back."

Too numb to reply, I crawled forward, horribly aware of how my soaked klút clung to my backside, wet in places, caked dry in others. Dutifully, I added a log to the fire, the wood prickly on my soft fingers. The room narrowed to that little pool of life-giving light.

"Jenna." Harlan sounded horrified, standing somewhere behind me. I bent my face to my knees. "Jenna—you're bleeding." He said it more loudly, then moved up beside me, holding up the saddle blanket, the firelight revealing circles of blood, dark and dried on the rim, bright in the middle.

I only looked away, then nodded. Unbearable to see my little brother holding the fouled thing. "I'm sorry," I whispered.

"Sorry?" His voice, normally so deep, rose into that squeak of emotion. "Don't be sorry. Just... why didn't you tell me?"

"There's nothing you can do." I sounded dull to myself. Maybe I'd lost too much blood. I wasn't even sure which parts of me were bleeding the most, it all hurt so much.

He folded himself to the rug beside me, putting his head in his hands. "I don't know anything about women," he admitted, his voice muffled. "I've heard things, though, that women, um… bleed sometimes, because of babies. Is that what this is?"

I laughed, feeling the bubble of hysteria rise in it. If only. "No. This isn't that."

"Then what?" He lifted his face and seized my wrist, making me look at him. "What did he do to you?"

I stared into Harlan's kind gray eyes, so anxious—afraid, even, when he hadn't shown any fear thus far—and found myself weeping, tears spilling down my face. "He hurt me," I said. Was all I could say.

Harlan let me go, closing his eyes and scrubbing a hand over his face. "And I made you sit astride a horse. I'm the one who's sorry. I'm a fool. *Stupid*!"

"No." I managed to say it forcefully enough, gathering myself and sniffing up the foolish tears. "You're smart, and clever, and so brave. You rescued me. Look—we've escaped!"

He shook his head. "Not yet. We're still much too close. The snow should make it hard to track us, and they won't expect us to have gone deeper into the mountains, but we won't be safe until we're truly away. And now I know how… injured you are. I don't know. Maybe we should just stay here and take our chances."

I was already shaking my head. Of course they'd chase us. We had to get far enough away that they couldn't find us. "We keep going," I said. "Or I will and you can go back to the Imperial Palace."

"Jenna." Harlan searched my face. "I'm not leaving you, but you have to think about this. That's a lot of blood. You could die."

I reached over and ruffled his hair, the impulse an old one, from when we were children. "If I'd stayed with Rodolf, I would have died. So every moment I have when he can't touch me is a moment I treasure."

He regarded me solemnly. "All right. I understand that. I'll melt some snow for drinking, and we can eat. Then we'll melt more and get you cleaned up."

"That's not necessary—"

"It is," he broke in, firmly but with that innate compassion. I had no idea where that came from, in our shark-infested family, but Helva had it, too. "I know it's embarrassing for both of us, but we're all the other has right now. You'll let me help you."

"I don't need it. It will heal on its own."

"Jenna…" He grimaced. "There are wolves in these forests and hills. They'll smell the blood. We have to deal with it."

Oh. Well… oh. So many ways I was stupid in the outside. Wolves who smelled blood—who knew?

"Let's eat," I agreed. "Then I'll bathe myself and… we'll see."

~ 18 ~

We struggled through it, my baby brother and I. It turned out that Harlan knew a little about rudimentary healing—how to seal up the worst cuts and so forth—though he cursed himself for not knowing more. "First thing I'm doing when we're somewhere safe," he told me at one point with a grim smile, "is learning more about both healing and women."

"You shouldn't need to know it ever again," I pointed out. My embarrassment and shame had reached a point where I'd passed into another kind of numbness.

"Sure I will. If I'm going to earn a living with my sword arm, then I'll have to know how to put people back together again, too. Especially if I have other men working for me."

"Working for you? You're an Imperial Prince—you'll command them."

He shook his head. "Not where we're going, I won't be a prince. In fact, we're safer if we don't tell anyone who we are. I'm thinking to hire as a mercenary. You can do that in Halabahna."

"Halabahna?" I echoed.

"That's where they have elephants." He grinned at me. "And it's not in the empire, so that's all I need. I'm thinking I can learn how to be a mercenary, earn coin that way to support us, and then I'll start my own company. This is all good experience."

"Well, you should at least never have to deal with a woman's body this way again." I'd taken strips of the ruined klút and rolled them up inside me, as I would during my woman's time, and we'd stopped the other bleeding. I was clean, and dressed in another set of Harlan's clothes. It felt odd to wear a shirt and pants—especially ones so oversized—but I used my many scarves to cinch them up enough so they wouldn't fall off.

"Sure I will. I want to be married someday. What kind of husband would I be if I didn't know how to take care of my wife? I'll need to know how to pleasure her, and stuff."

"Oh, Harlan." I had no idea what to say to him. "Don't they…" Impossibly I blushed, even after our horrible enforced intimacy. "Give you lessons?"

"No." He paused in feeding the remains of the ruined klút into the fire. "Did you get lessons?"

I nodded. "I feel weird having this conversation with my brother."

He grinned, full of his good-hearted nature. "I think we've already shared more than most siblings do. Don't hold out on me. What lessons did you get?"

I waved a hand vaguely. "Sex. How to pleasure a man. How everything … works."

He gazed at me, astounded. "So not fair. We don't get lessons. Well, not yet, anyway," he amended. "That might have been the fifteenth birthday deal."

"The deal?" I laughed. I felt surprisingly good. Of course, I'd had a fair amount of mjed, and I'd slept awhile. I was warm and clean. Soon it would be full dark and we'd move on.

Harlan's smile went crooked. "When a guy turns fifteen there's some kind of party. The rekjabrel were teasing me about it, saying how they planned to volunteer for mine. I think I now get some of the jokes."

"Your birthday is late autumn," I remembered.

"Yeah." He poked at the fire, stirring the logs so the fabric all burned away. "No rekjabrel party for me."

"You can still go back. Say that I escaped and you chased me, but I got away."

"I'm not going back, Jenna. And I'm not sad about missing that party. I'd rather my first time be with a woman who actually likes me, you know? Not because she has to choose between pleasuring me or some other guy that night."

"It's not always that way," I started, but I wasn't sure that was the truth.

Harlan was watching me. "Maybe not always. But it is often enough that I wouldn't have felt right. Now that I've seen… Well, I only wish I'd been able to run Rodolf through with a spear and slow roast him over a fire." His genial face, once so earnest and full of warmth, had contorted into something grim and dark. "And they all knew what he was doing to you. Do you think I'd willingly go back to that—be a part of that?"

He looked so fierce, both enraged and wounded at once, that I went to him and embraced him. Awkwardly, he returned the hug, holding me gently. Younger than I was, but already bigger and stronger. I tipped my head back to look at him.

"No," I said. "You wouldn't. You're a fine man, Harlan, and whatever woman earns your heart someday, she'll be the luckiest woman in the world. I'm going to make sure she knows that."

* * * *

When we left our little cabin at dark—after Harlan tossed the hot coals into the snow and laid fresh kindling for the next travelers to easily light a fire—I rode sideways across Harlan's lap. It wasn't ideal, but he wouldn't hear of anything else. That way we wrapped both cloaks around us, which made us warmer.

A good thing, as we headed up the mountain, deeper snow, colder temperatures, and cruelly whipping winds. It was best that way, Harlan explained, as Rodolf wouldn't expect it of either of us. He'd hopefully waste time chasing us back to the Imperial Palace—or down to Jofarstyrr, if he thought we might try to lose ourselves in the city, or to buy passage on one of the many ships in the harbor there.

"The one thing in our favor these first few days," Harlan said, "is that Rodolf is a proud man. He won't want to admit to the emperor—or anyone, really—that he's lost you." Harlan hadn't referred to the man as my husband since that first night in the cabin. Nor had I.

According to Dasnarian law, however, he was my husband in fact and would remain so until one or the other of us died. I didn't have the education to know what that might mean if I managed to leave the Dasnarian Empire, but I wanted my exile from Dasnaria and its laws to mean my exit from the vows of marriage. Something to think about later.

We stayed in another cabin come the gray light of morning, much the same as the first. For travelers and hunters, Harlan explained. A tradition in this part of the empire, where sudden blizzards could strand people for days. We never saw any of these other people. I finally figured out that Harlan was carefully keeping clear of encountering any. We kept to the woods, where the evergreen canopy prevented the snow from being so deep, following what Harlan called deer trails.

The first time I saw actual deer, I nearly scared Harlan off the horse. The dark silhouettes ran across our trail, liquid and fleet. I squealed with surprise and delight—and our mount lifted his head and whinnied. Fortunately Harlan recovered quickly, realizing I wasn't sounding an alarm. He reined up, and we watched them pass. One stopped, elegant and intricate antlers an echo of the tangled black branches above, the filtered moonlight silvering its fur so it looked made of more snow. A wild thing of the forest, with dark, glistening eyes that seemed to hold the wisdom I lacked.

"Just deer," Harlan said, wrapping an arm around me and squeezing. "Nothing to fear."

"I know. I've never seen them before. The outside is so much huger than I ever understood, where these creatures wander about, wild and free."

He was quiet a while after that, but began pointing out various wildlife to me. An owl watching us solemnly from a tree. The tracks of rabbits and wolves in the snow. I didn't say it, because I knew he'd think I was crazy—which, admittedly, I might have been a little, in my exhaustion, shock, and entirely shattered state of mind—but I hoped to see the wolves, too.

The third cabin we stopped at, we barely made it to through a blizzard so howling dense with snow we nearly missed it. That one had a cozy stable for the horses with plenty of hay—that scratchy plant stuff I'd crouched in that night we escaped—and even some grain. I'd learned how to start the fire, so I did that while Harlan settled the horses. When he came in, he gave me a broad smile and showed me a quarter of venison that had been frozen and kept in a small cellar along with some potatoes.

He hacked off chunks of frozen meat and we boiled it all into a thick stew, which we ate so hot it burned our mouths. A welcome change from the cold rations Harlan had packed for our escape. Then we slept. All the remaining day and through the night. I warmed up the leftover stew while Harlan checked the horses. He came back saying that the snow had fallen so deep we might as well stay another day. So I made more stew, and we stuffed ourselves again and slept more.

By the time the storm cleared and we left, we both felt rested. And I felt human again. Not only because I got to see the sun. Astonishingly bright, it glittered off the snow that covered everything, scorchingly brilliant and cold. The sky shone with a blueness like I'd never seen. And the days of rest had let me heal enough to try sitting astride. Harlan gave me lessons on sitting a horse, how to hold on with my legs and not my hands.

A lot of it was not being afraid—not easy for me. I jumped at the least thing anymore, and—though I'd found a place of equanimity—the rime of fear that Rodolf would find me ran through my blood. But my mare was a pretty thing, chosen for her dark hide and amiable nature, as well as her sturdy mountain-climbing build. She mistrusted my scarves, and I learned to tie the ends in tightly so they wouldn't flutter. Otherwise she tolerated my poor technique. In return, I let her follow Harlan's horse, which made her happy enough.

In another day, we descended over a gentle ridge to find warmer wind blowing in our faces. It smelled different than the mountain air, a hint of salt and the fish we occasionally ate in the seraglio. Harlan reined up and pointed. I looked, trying to understand what he showed me. The mountains fell away into hills beneath us. Beyond them, the land lay flat and featureless, a uniform dark gray. A dot glided across it and I frowned.

Then I understood in a rush of awed astonishment. "Is that the *ocean*?" I asked.

Harlan grinned over his shoulder at me and nodded. "I remember the first time I saw it, too. Not like you expect, is it?"

"No." I'd expected blue water and palm trees, like the paintings on the walls in the seraglio. As with the deer, the reality of the ocean was magnitudes beyond the images I'd been shown. It stretched out farther than I could see, immense and with a power that made me feel even smaller than I'd come to understand myself to be. Once I'd been an Imperial Princess, reigning over my limited empire, thinking myself something beyond special.

Now, in Harlan's castoff boy's clothes, stripped of my jewels—the ones I could liberate myself from—filthy and soon to be an exile from everything I'd known, I knew myself to be immeasurably tiny. And without worth, unless I made myself into something more.

We rode down through valleys, growing warmer as we went, the snow thinning and wildlife increasing. Deer and elk thundered past in great herds. Birds flocked in chorusing flights overhead. Finding a travelers cabin in late afternoon, we stopped early. We'd eat the last of our cold rations, as the next day we'd ride into the harbor city of Sjør, and seek a ship to sail to Halabahna.

"Jenna," Harlan said in a serious voice, seating himself beside me. I knew that tone, the one that would convey unpleasant news. "We need to see about removing your ring and wedding bracelets."

"Good," I replied, and held out my hands. He looked nonplussed, so I laughed. "Did you think I'd mind? The cursed things are like shackles. I'd love to be free of them."

"It's not that." He gathered my hands in his. "Believe me, I understand. The thing is…I don't have the tools. We need a metalworker to break them open."

"Oh." Which meant I'd be recognized. "Then leave them on. I can cover them with scarves and we can find someone in Sjør to do it."

Harlan scrubbed a hand over his scalp. "It's too great a risk. If word has made it to Sjør, then people might be watching for someone disguising bracelets like this—and the ring is showy. Too easy to slip and have it catch the eye. One glimpse of a diamond like that and everyone will know you're no commoner. Women traveling abroad are rare enough. One as beautiful as you with such gems…"

I nodded. "We could cut my hands off," I offered, not entirely joking. I'd be willing to pay that price.

Harlan, however, looked horrified. "I think we can avoid that. We should, however, cut off your hair. And dye it darker."

My hair. Of course. "All right."

A strange smile twisted his mouth. "Just like that?"

"I've lost more of myself than hair," I replied, matter-of-factly. *Only flesh.* "I'm not who I was, so fine. Do you have a knife appropriate for this purpose?" I'd been learning knives; which were for chopping food, which for plants, which to keep clean and sharp for fighting.

"I can do it for you," Harlan offered, pulling out the sharp meat-cutting knife.

"No," I replied. "I want to do it."

I had my hair tied back in a single long braid—the same I'd put it in that night at the seraglio. My braid for sleeping, that I hadn't taken down as I had no way to wash my hair or comb it out. Taking the knife, I slipped the blade under the tie at the back of my neck, the metal cool and smooth, then sawed upward.

Short hairs came free as I cut, billowing and blowing around my face in that ever-present breeze off the ocean. The braid came free and my scalp tingled with lightness, my head feeling as if it could float off my neck. Harlan watched me with a strange expression, then held out his hand. I gave him his knife back.

"The braid," he asked, "could I keep it?"

"If you want to." I handed him the long rope of ivory hair. Not sleek or lovely, not interwoven with pearls. Hairs stood out in branchy brambles. It looked like nothing of mine. Harlan carefully tied off the free end, coiled it up and put it in one of his packs, and I ran my fingers through the short fluff of hair, marveling at the sensation. "Why do you want it?"

Harlan gave me a kind of sideways look. "Superstitious, maybe. It seems wrong not to."

I'd have thrown it on the fire, but such was my state of mind. "And dying what remains?"

He shook his head thoughtfully, studying me. "I've changed my mind on that. Dasnarian women are mostly fair-haired, so if we dyed it dark you'd stand out more. And with it so chopped off... well, you look nothing like Imperial Princess Jenna."

I smiled at that. "Good."

Because I wasn't her anymore. Once I'd shed Rodolf's jeweled manacles, I'd be free of the last vestiges of the stupid, helpless girl I'd been.

Then maybe I could start becoming someone else.

~ 19 ~

We rode down into the harbor city of Sjør the next morning. The back way, sadly, which was more circumspect, but just as thrilling. A real city. Harlan had told me there wouldn't be much to see. He'd explained apologetically, coming from the woods, down the country lanes and past the little farms that gradually clustered together, that there would be other cities, other bright mornings, when I could ride down the main thoroughfare and drink in the sight of the sailing ships and merchants selling all manner of things from their handcarts, not just glimpses between houses.

But I loved every small glimpse, every sight so tame to Harlan's experienced eye. I drank every bit of it in, thirsty for more, and Harlan had to keep reminding me not to look about like a country mouse seeing the city for the first time. Even though that's exactly what I was.

Still, I mostly managed to remember to keep my head down, face hidden beneath the cowl of my cloak. I had wrapped my hands in the heavier scarves, so none would see. We took a roundabout route to a denser, smellier part of the city, where men called blacksmiths worked at blistering fires that belched smoke, metal ringing loud as they worked it.

We stopped at several, Harlan having me wait while he went in. Each time he came out, shaking his head. "Why not that one?" I asked, after the fourth time.

"I'm looking for a particular type," Harlan explained. "A man honest enough to do the job and not look to make more by selling us out; and yet dishonest enough to take the bribe in the first place."

I considered that. It made sense, and yet... "How can you determine that?"

Harlan grimaced. "I ask them if they'll reshoe my horse—and I'll let them keep the higher quality shoes in exchange."

"I don't understand."

"Our horses were shod at Castle Fjaltyndar. I'm obviously no prince of that castle, to their eye, so they assume I've stolen them and look to cover the crime by changing the shoes."

"Ah." I nodded. "And little do they know that the stolen property to be stripped of identifying equipment is actually me."

He glanced at me, frowning. "I didn't mean it that way."

I lifted a shoulder and let it fall, as I'd seen Harlan often do. "I'm not offended. I'm well aware of my relative status in the world I'm leaving behind. So these men have all refused?"

"Actually, no—they agreed too easily, and with greed in their eye. I don't trust any of them with you, so we keep looking."

"What if they alert the guard that a man is trying to reshoe stolen horses?"

"It's possible, but the city guard isn't like at the Imp—where we came from," he amended, as a group of farmers passed us, pulling a wagon with a broken wheel. "They are spread thin and kept busy with existing problems. They're unlikely to chase down a possible problem, guessed at by a blacksmith who never examined the shoes in question."

We passed a blacksmith shop smaller than the others, but neatly kept. Three young girls played in the dusty yard, two chasing a round spinning toy they drove with strikes of a stick, and the other sitting in the sun, intent on something she worked with her hands. They all looked clean and well-fed, barefoot with pretty bangles jingling on their ankles, but too young for klúts yet. As I watched, the one who'd been working on something jumped up, ran over to a man working the forge, and showed him. He took it, nodding, then patted her on the shoulder.

"That place," I told Harlan, pointing with my chin.

He squinted in that direction. "It doesn't look like much."

"We don't need much."

"Why that one?"

"He's good to his daughter." *He's letting her do something useful*, I didn't add, but I continued to watch as the man showed the girl something.

"As good a criterion as any," Harlan agreed. "Wait here."

But I didn't. Fully aware that I disobeyed him—and feeling a little thrill in the doing, as apparently rebellions feed each other, making each one easier—I allowed my mare to follow after his horse, into the yard. The two younger girls stopped in their play, observing us with curiosity but no fear. A woman dressed in a simple klút, tucked up high for chores, appeared in the doorway of the attached house and called to them to come help her. She waved to us in greeting, gaze averted enough to be polite, but not so much that she didn't look us over. She had an easy smile and moved with the supple energy of a happy woman.

The blacksmith sent the older girl inside, too, as Harlan approached, and she took me in more boldly, likely wondering at my heavy cloak in the warm sunshine. Harlan and the blacksmith still talked, the man shaking his head, casting a dubious eye at our horses. Too honest.

Making a decision—as this was my choice, ultimately—I dismounted and clomped my way through the dirt to the men. The blacksmith nodded me a greeting, respectfully enough, and spoke to me, too. "Well met, young lord," he said, "but I've told your companion here, while I sympathize with your plight, I cannot help you. I have a family to think of."

I nodded back, understanding. Instead I turned my back to the street, opened my cloak and began unwinding a scarf from my left hand. Harlan gripped my forearm. "No," he whispered, a harsh warning. "We'll find someone else."

"I trust this man," I told him. "I have to start trusting somewhere. Surely not every man is my enemy."

Harlan shook his head, but let me go. The blacksmith looked between us curiously. I pulled the cloth aside enough to show him the edge of the jewel-encrusted bracelet. His breath hissed out, and his gaze went to my shadowed face, which I lifted enough for him to see.

"I need you to cut off my wedding bracelets. In exchange you may keep one. As you can see, they're valuable."

He leaned a hand on his workbench, lowering his head, shaking it as if he had an earache. "You're her. The lost princess."

Harlan put his hand to his sword, ready to draw. I hoped it wouldn't come to that, with this honest man and his happy family.

"Yes. I wish only to flee, not to cause any trouble. If you won't do this, I understand. We'll leave and never bother you. But I'm asking you to help me."

"You're leaving the empire?" He asked, disbelief and horror hushing his voice further. "Why? Your people love you. You have everything."

I unwound the scarf a bit more and slid the bracelet down, showing him the marks the cuffs left on me, the deep bruises that had yet to heal fully, shadowing the pink ridged skin where the deep cuts worked to become scars. "He hurt me," I told the blacksmith, willing him to understand all the details I couldn't bear to say. "If this isn't enough to convince you,

I'll undress for your wife and she can bear witness to …" I swallowed. "To my other injuries."

He wouldn't look at me, pained tension ridging his shoulders. "And who are you—her lover?" he asked Harlan.

"He's my brother," I answered for him. "He's risked his life and future to help me."

The blacksmith fully gaped now, knees flexing instinctively. "You're one of the Imperial Princes! Forgive me, Your—"

Harlan gripped him by the shoulder, stopping him—an incongruous sight, with my little brother shorter and slighter than the big blacksmith. "Not anymore," Harlan said quietly, and firmly, full of resolve. "I've resigned my rank. I'm no more royal than you."

The blacksmith breathed a laugh. "I don't believe it will be so easy, young lord, but so be it." He gripped Harlan's shoulder in return, then faced me. "The law says a man may do with his wife as he will, but I'd eviscerate any vámr who treated a woman so. Let's go in the house. I don't need the forge for this and we're better away from curious eyes."

* * * *

I sat at the table where the family normally ate, all together, apparently, as there were six chairs—always an extra for visitors, the wife told me with a cheerful smile—set in the middle of their pretty, cozy home. With windows all around that let the sunshine in.

The blacksmith took his wife aside, explaining in a low voice. She paled beneath her healthy tan, glancing at me with trepidation, then nodded decisively, coming over to me. "May I take your cloak, Your—"

"Just Jenna," I interrupted, adding a smile to soften it. I wondered then if I should change my name entirely. No reason not to give up everything of who I'd been.

"Our eldest is also Jenna. Named for the Imperial Princess, you know." She winked at me. "So many girls with that name now, but it's so pretty. Auspicious, too, to be named for the pearl of the empire. I am Rillian."

"It's lovely to meet you," I told her, letting her take the much-too-warm cloak, and sitting where she gestured at the table. The blacksmith had gone to fetch his tools, and Harlan stood outside, apparently checking our tack, but keeping an eye out for trouble. I didn't know where the little girls had gone.

"Would you care for something to eat or drink?" Rillian offered.

"No, I won't trouble you more than I am already."

"It's no trouble," she replied crisply, eyes on the wounds I revealed as I finished unknotting the scarves. "Brian shouldn't have hesitated. This is what any decent person would do."

"It is trouble," Brian corrected, entering the room, tools in one hand and the oldest girl snugged against his side with the other. "But we're doing it anyway because it is the decent thing to do. Right, Jenna?"

I nearly answered, then realized he meant his daughter, for she looked up at him with an admiring smile, as if he were the sun of her universe. "Right, Daddy."

"Jenna," Rillian began, "why don't you—"

"I want her to see this," Brian cut in. "The littles are playing."

"She's only thirteen…"

"And I see the neighborhood boys making eyes at her. Don't they?" He turned a fierce gaze on young Jenna, who giggled nervously. "She needs to know what can happen, if she doesn't choose wisely."

Jenna edged over and sat across from me, eyes wide and dark on my hands, where I laid them on the table. The jewels glittered with cold beauty, merciless contrast to the bruised and battered flesh they encased. She raised her eyes to mine. "Did you not choose wisely?"

"I didn't have a choice," I told her.

"But… you're an Imperial Princess!" She lowered her voice when her mother hushed her. "You can do anything."

Brian inspected the bracelet on my left hand, shaking his head. "I'll have to saw it off. This kind of lock, once engaged, is designed to be unbreakable."

"Whatever you need to do."

He grunted, attaching an implement to the table edge, then clamping my bracelet in it. "Hold still—the vise will help—and I ought to be able to avoid your skin." With a long, thin serrated blade, he began sawing at the metal on a side away from the heavy clasp.

"You're right," I said to Jenna. Rillian sat beside her, an arm around her daughter, who looked terribly unhappy. "I went along with everything because other people told me to. I could have refused."

"Could you have?" Rillian asked, her expression somber. "Not without great difficulty, I think."

I inclined my head. "Would they have forced me? Perhaps. But I have difficulty now. If I could go back—" I shook that thought away, focusing on young Jenna. "That's the thing about choosing wisely. We don't get to go back and change the past."

Brian gave a grunt of satisfaction, releasing me from the vise. He took the bracelet in both his big hands, pulling it wider, and I slipped my hand free. Free. A diamond popped from its setting and went bouncing. Jenna scrambled to fetch it, holding it up to the light as Brian moved to my other side, reattaching the vise to the table.

"Is this real?" Young Jenna breathed.

"Yes. And it's yours now."

"Oh, no," Rillian exclaimed. "We can't possibly."

"We can and we will," Brian said, beginning to saw on the other bracelet. "That's the deal—we keep that one."

"And do what with it?" she demanded. "This is a fortune in Imperial jewels. Are we to buy meat and fabric with diamonds?"

Brian looked up at her. "No. We take our savings and use it to buy passage back to Myli. You've been wanting to go home anyway. Your family will help us sell the gems, little by little."

"Brian..." Rillian sounded both broken and full of hope. "Truly?"

"It's a better place for the girls," he replied, head down, sawing with meticulous care. "You're right. This is no place for them to grow up. With these gems, they'll have good dowries. Better than good. We can provide for your parents—I know you've worried about them. There."

He picked up a pair of heavy shears and snapped the little chains to the diamond ring, then wedged open the bracelet for me to slip my hand out. When the ring wouldn't come off, Rillian fetched me some soap and water, working it gently until it, too, relinquished its hold on me.

Because young Jenna stared at the ostentatious diamond with such fascination, I handed it to her to look at. Then turned to Rillian, and Brian, carefully replacing his tools in a leather packet. "Thank you," I told them. "I don't imagine I'll ever be in a position to do much for anyone, but I am forever in your debt."

"You're not," Rillian said firmly, taking the ring from Jenna and giving it back to me. She let her keep the smaller diamond, though, and wrapped up the one bracelet in a towel for washing dishes. "We'll do as Brian says—just pack up and leave, today, if we can manage it."

Brian nodded. "I've already turned off the forge. Anything we can't carry, we'll leave and replace in Myli."

"I'm having that diamond set for you," Rillian said to young Jenna. "So you can wear it around your neck and remember your namesake, remember what a true princess is like. Courageous and full of kindness and grace, even under the worst circumstances."

Tears spilled out of my eyes. "No, wait," I said, shaking my head when young Jenna made to hand the diamond back to me. I dug out one of my gloves from a deep pocket in the cloak, and worried off one of the biggest pearls. "Sell the diamonds. For a remembrance, keep this."

Jenna held it with wonder, rolling it in her palm.

"Wear it against your skin," I advised her. "Pearls need that."

Rillian took my hand, squeezing it. "We wish you the best—and I, personally, expect to hear of great deeds from you in the future."

~ 20 ~

Harlan used the last of his coin to buy us passage on a ship leaving on the morning tide for the port city at Halabahna. Better to save the oh-so-recognizable gems and precious metal for bartering in Halabahna once we arrived. And he found us a room at an inn. The smell and sounds of the bustling place reminded me searingly of the one before, where Rodolf had served me his final lessons, but I'd bear it for the night.

It wasn't a bad omen. Just because he'd told me I could never escape him, that he'd kill Harlan before my eyes if I tried, that didn't mean he could. I *had* escaped him. And I was free of his cursed ring and bracelets. In a sort of wonder, my fingers kept straying to my unburdened wrists, rubbing the healing skin, the scars I'd always bear.

I stayed in our shared room, hiding away from sight, as did Harlan. He sent servants after food and drink, and to fill a bath for us, setting up a screen for privacy. Once they left us alone, we both shed our cloaks with relief.

"You go first," Harlan told me. "We might as well get clean now, as we won't likely have the opportunity on the journey."

"You shouldn't have to take my used water," I protested.

"Then wash fast, so it's not all cold." He gave me a cheerful grin and went to stir the fire.

Without delay, I shed my clothes, beyond delighted to sink into the hot water. The journey to Halabahna would take fully ten days, and we'd share a cabin, traveling as brothers. Best for no one to suspect my gender, Harlan thought, not until we'd made it well clear of the Dasnarian Empire's reach.

He didn't know how it was for women in Halabahna, if they could handle money or walk about without male escort, so he also thought it best for me to maintain a boyish disguise even after we disembarked in the port city. If we didn't like it there, we'd go somewhere else. After we saw real live elephants, he added, with a happy grin.

We were both in good spirits, feeling celebratory, despite the lingering chill of fear. That might chase me for a long time, maybe all my life. I refused, however, to let superstition rule me. We'd made it thus far with no sign of pursuit. Probably Rodolf still scoured the trade routes on the other side of the mountains, thinking I could never be so audacious as to cross in midwinter.

But I had done it. I was stronger than he knew.

I'd bathed, dried off, and dressed again, nibbling at the enticing smelling roast fowl while Harlan took his turn in the tub, when a knock came at the door. My heart climbed to my throat, and Harlan clambered out of the tub, calling out that we were fine and needed nothing.

The door crashed open, the wood splintering around the bolt.

Kral stood there, surrounded by Imperial guards.

I stared at him, completely dumbfounded, unable to make myself move. His icy blue gaze raked me, and he smiled thinly as he took in my ragged hair and the boy's clothes I'd put back on, then to Harlan, dripping wet and wrapped only in a towel—but sword in hand.

"Don't," Kral said softly as Harlan moved to interpose himself between me and Kral. His own sword in hand, fully armored, Kral advanced on Harlan, pointing the lethal tip at him. "Don't make me kill you when I'm fully prepared to forgive. As is our father." He looked between us. "Both of you, if you come home with me. Leave us," he told the guards. "Remain on the door and at the windows below. Smells good," he added with that same lethal smile. "Shall we eat and talk?"

* * * *

A strange meal, for the three of us to sit at a table together. Kral allowed Harlan to don his pants but nothing else, also making him leave his weapons on the other side of the room, whereas he kept on his armor, sheathing his sword but keeping his long knife across his lap.

I thought about seizing it, if only to cut my own throat, but I wasn't sure I could move fast enough. Sick to my stomach, I couldn't eat. Neither did Harlan, watching me across the table with gray eyes full of an intense message I couldn't read.

For his part, Kral ate with enthusiasm, complaining only about the lack of wine or mjed. When he'd stuffed himself, he sat back, surveying us. "So."

"How did you find us?" Harlan asked, in the same neutral tone.

Kral's eyes flashed with, of all things, humor. "Because you're stupid, little rabbit." He shook his head. "You have growing up to do, letting sentiment lead you. This is the only port city close enough with ships going to Halabahna, and we all remember the fits little Jenna here had about seeing an elephant. You made yourself sick over it, remember?" he asked me.

I didn't reply, regarding him steadily. Of course he had no idea what our mother had done to me, making me sick. But he was right that we'd let sentiment lead us to such an obvious choice. Of course, we had expected Rodolf to chase us, not our own brother. And I knew precious little of the world.

If I survived, I would change that.

"All I had to do was wait here and watch the inns." Kral let his gaze wander over my face, taking in the marks on my arms I didn't try to hide. "Though I admit I almost missed you, the way you look now. What have you done to yourself?" He asked. "Your beautiful hair."

I laughed, the sound harsh enough to make him flinch. "What about my beautiful skin—don't you miss that, too? This is Rodolf's work."

To his credit, he cringed a little, then shook his head. "We all bear wounds in battle. Did you think your fairer sex entitled you to coddling? Our mother would never have run away like this. Not with everything we have riding on it." His gaze flicked to Harlan and away. "You knew how important this was."

"What?" I prodded. I might not have any weapons, but I did possess our family secrets—and I'd lost any loyalty or reason to keep them for the people who'd destroy me for their ambitions. "You don't want Harlan to know how our mother conspired with the Elskadyrs and Rodolf to make me Queen of Arynherk, so they could unseat our father from the throne of the empire?"

Harlan sat up straighter. "Hulda... did what?"

I ignored Kral's scowl of warning. "That was the deal. I'd marry and the Elskadyrs would back Rodolf in a rebellion. He planned to be emperor, did you know that?" I asked Kral, who shook his head, jaw tight.

"No, your son would have been emperor and I was to be regent."

"Not if Rodolf killed me," I corrected, full of fiery vengeance. "Did you know that part?" Kral gazed at me in dawning horror and I nodded at him. "Makes sense, doesn't it. Rodolf would kill me, our father would move to punish him..."

"And the Elskadyrs would have first backed Rodolf until he committed his forces, then abandoned him to put me on the throne instead," Kral finished. "I didn't know that part, but certain things Mother said make sense now."

"How could you do it?" I asked him. "How could you sit by while that monster—"

"I didn't know, all right?" Kral fired back. "Besides, it's over now. Father promised that if I bring you back—both of you—then he'll make me heir instead of Hestar. We'll have everything we worked for."

Harlan and I exchanged long looks.

"Now you know," I told him softly. "If you need them, the secrets will give you power."

"I'll protect you both," Kral protested. "I'll be heir. I'll have the power to do that."

"Do you really believe him?" Harlan asked. "Hestar is the image of our father in every way. His pride, his creation. Hestar has been heir since his birth."

"Well, that's changing," Kral snapped. "His Imperial Majesty vowed to me and the empress, that if I deliver you two home, then I will be heir. Mother is overjoyed—and asked me to tell you she misses you and can't wait to have you home where you belong," he added to me. "Though she's angry that you flaunted the law and fled from your husband, she—"

"That man is not my husband," I interrupted, unwilling to hear another word of that pap. I held up my unshackled wrists. "I divorced him."

Kral's lips parted, his astonishment almost comical. "You can't divorce your husband," he replied, finally finding his voice.

"I'm an Imperial Princess," I retorted. "I can do whatever I want to do."

"Not anymore, you're not," he fired back.

"No? Good. Then the Imperial Palace is not my home, I owe no loyalty to you or our parents, and I'm not going back."

Kral's jaw tightened. "You're still a subject of the Dasnarian Empire and I'm an Imperial Prince. You will obey me."

I lifted a shoulder and let it fall. "No."

His lip curled in frustration, flingers flexing. "You've changed, Jenna."

"Thank you." The smile broke across my face, and I had to laugh. "Thank you, Brother. I'm delighted to hear that."

"It wasn't a compliment," he snarled. "And, in case the two of you idiots missed it, you're surrounded by Imperial Guards. You're going back with me if I have to hogtie you and cart you in a wagon."

"Don't do this, Kral." Impulsively, I seized his hand with both of mine. "Come with us. We're going to build a new life, far away from the manipulations of our mother and the power madness of the emperor. Hulda used me in the worst way for her own ambition and she's doing the same to you. You'll never be happy there."

He yanked his hand from my grip. "There's more to life than being happy. I'm going to be Emperor!"

"You're not." I shook my head, sorry for his blindness. For what our mother had done to him, too. "She'll betray you, too. Seize something for yourself, make your own life!"

"Fools," Kral growled. "I don't know how I'm related to you." He pushed back from the table and stood. "Harlan, you'll share my room, where I can keep an eye on you. It's not seemly to share a room with our sister. Be glad no one knows of your presence here. Jenna, get some sleep. The guards will remain outside to keep you safe. Have you any proper clothing?"

I shook my head, and he looked disgusted. "I'll find a klút for you to wear. Where are your bracelets and ring?"

"I threw them in the ocean," I lied, head high.

You'd think he'd have been done being surprised by me, but no. "A fortune in jewels and she throws them in the ocean." He shook his head in amazement. "I know women aren't the intellectual equals of men, but even that is beyond stupidity."

"I only worry some innocent fish will choke on the cursed things," I replied.

"I'll arrange for a klút and a maid for morning," he said, gathering Harlan's weapons and gesturing him out the door. "Maybe she can do something with your hair. Be ready to leave."

From the doorway, Harlan gave me a long look, then a salute with the tips of his fingers to his temple.

~ 21 ~

I didn't sleep. Who could?

Instead I added to my already complicated relationship with inns by pacing the floor. Like and unlike that night I spent with Rodolf. Once again, I was trapped in a room not mine, locked in with terror of the future for close company. This time, however, I wasn't gagged or bound. And I no longer wore Rodolf's chains of ownership.

The only person keeping me in that room was me.

Yes, there were the guards outside, but still—I was deciding to stay put, wasn't I? Waiting for morning and for Kral and to be groomed to be who they wanted me to be. No Harlan to rescue me this time. *Do you need to be rescued?* I did, and the only person who could do that was me.

I'd come so far. Not eight locked doors between me and the outside, only one. And a window.

With no one there to tell me I couldn't look out of it.

So I doused all my lanterns, went to the window, and opened it. Just like that. This kind had hinges on one side, like a door, so it swung open, leaving nothing between me and the chilly night air. Colder than the day with its warm sunshine, but still so much warmer than the frozen mountains. The inn sat on a back street—cheaper and more inconspicuous, Harlan had said—so I couldn't see the harbor, only rows of darkened buildings, and an empty street winding between them.

I'd expected to see the Imperial Guards standing at attention, as they had all over the Imperial Palace, but I couldn't spot them at all. I leaned out, craning to see, and finally spotted them to the side of the front doors to the inn. Lanterns turned low flanked the doors, and a pair of guards sat with the boy who'd taken our horses when we arrived. They seemed to be intent on some game, all bent over it. One of the guards picked up a pitcher from the ground and refilled their mugs. Wine or mjed, it had to be.

They weren't even watching my window. My heart thudded with real excitement, with possibility. Of course they didn't expect me to cause trouble. What woman would? And they all knew I'd only escaped because Harlan broke me out of the seraglio. They figured me for sleeping and docilely waiting to be dressed and carted home. In their minds, the emperor's wayward property had already been retrieved, nothing more than another bag of valuables to load into the carriages in the morning.

But I had legs—strong dancer's legs—and the determination of my bloodline. Kral was no smarter than I was, just more educated and experienced in the world. I could do this. That had been the message in Harlan's quiet gray gaze as Kral went on about his ambitions. He'd been telling me to go.

All alone. A woman without escort or protection. So I wouldn't be her. Exactly as we'd planned, I'd be a young man. Heading out to see the world. But not to Halabahna. That much was clear.

I stirred the fire, stoking the flames to light the room, and bundled up my things. I worried a couple of pearls off my glove. I put those in my trouser pockets—something else a klút didn't have, those handy pockets—and wrapped the gloves and bracelet in my scarves. Thinking of Rillian and her kitchen towel, I stuck that inside an innocuous-looking pouch we'd carried food in.

I wouldn't have food, but I'd figure out a way to get it. Everything was possible as long as I got away. Every decision I came to had to be made with freedom in mind.

The diamond ring I waffled over. I really wanted to leave it behind, a symbol of my divorce. They could give it back to Rodolf and he'd know I'd left it. Then again, it was beyond valuable and I'd certainly earned it. So valuable and ostentatious, however, that it would be easily identifiable. And I doubted I could use it to buy anything. Anything short of an entire kingdom and, well, that just might draw attention.

So I left it there. I even arranged the carcass of the roast fowl, with the bones sucked clean by Kral's voracious appetite, radiating out from the ring. The flawless gem sparkled amid the grease and rejected gristle. The only goodbye letter I was capable of leaving, but it said everything.

Who knew—maybe a servant would find it and keep the thing. Or accidentally throw it in the refuse. I didn't care. I'd said what I wanted to.

Really, though, I hoped Harlan would see it and smile, knowing that I was okay. That it was a goodbye.

Tying the few things I planned to take with me around my waist with extra scarves, I donned the dark, plain cloak, then scattered the logs and coals to dim the room again. Checking that the guards were still occupied—they were—I climbed out the window barefoot. I trusted the practiced grip of my toes better than the clunky boots, which I'd tied to my waist also.

I wondered what my mother would think to know that all the hours I'd practiced on my dances, the exquisite control I'd refined for the ducerse to make sure I could move without making any of the bells I wore jingle in the slightest, would allow me to climb silently out the second floor window of an inn, then glide across the pitched roof to the building next door.

I'm not sure I even felt afraid—I don't remember it. It's possible I'd grown so accustomed to fear that I didn't notice it anymore, like a foul smell that fades into the background. Mostly I felt exhilaration. I walked over several more roofs than I needed to, delighted that I could, that my feet found a grip on the corrugated tiles, and I moved without fluttering my cloak, making no sound.

In this, at least, I'd been well educated.

A cat passed me, going the other direction, also silently picking her way along the roofline. Her eyes flashed at me and I felt we nodded at each other, shadows passing in the night. I found an outside staircase and padded down it, keeping to the back alley where people set the things they didn't care for anyone to see.

Feeling like the only person awake in the entire world, I made my way down to the harbor, where the ships sat creaking at the docks. A brisk wind blew off the water, smelling of brine, distant storms, and my future.

Here there were people awake, sailors keeping watch or working on rigging. I stopped to pull on my boots. I could make noise again, and no man walked about barefoot. So many ships lined up—all along the extensive, curving harbor. Which had Harlan booked us passage on? Not that I'd board that ship, but if I could, I wanted his coin back.

And maybe to leave a message.

He'd told me the name of the ship, but I couldn't read the scrolling letters painted or carved into the wood of the proud vessels. Finally, I took the risk of asking a passing man if he knew which ship it was. I kept my voice low, making it a little hoarse, as if I suffered a sore throat.

The man squinted up one way, then the other. Pointing he told me the tenth ship down, with the red lanterns hanging off the sides. I didn't know ten, but I could find red, so I nodded and went that way. He went the other, a simple interaction for him, a momentous one for me. The first time I'd ever spoken to a strange man without an escort.

And nothing bad had happened to me. Still, I clutched the little eating knife under my cloak. I might not be able to do much damage with it—too small even to cut my own throat with, unless I sawed at it, and I doubted I could make myself do that, no matter my desperation—but Harlan had shown me how to grip a knife in my fist and go for the eye. That's what I'd do. I'd plunge it in, then jump off the dock and let myself drown.

I talked myself through it. The dense wool of the cloak would weigh me down, and I wouldn't fight for air. I'd sink, knowing I'd died free, if it came to that.

Thus, I realized, I'd already found freedom. I'd made my own choices, and nothing could send me back. No matter when I perished from the world, it would be as me, Jenna the free woman.

At the ship, sailors bustled about, clearly making ready to sail away. Though the sky remained as dark as before, it seemed dawn must be coming. More lanterns lit in windows. Some sounds came from town. Wheels on stone. A horse whinnying.

I walked up the sloping plank from the dock to the ship, letting my boots clomp. A sailor noticed me. "Passenger?"

"Yeh," I said, imitating the man I'd talked to. "The captain?"

"There." He pointed to a heavy man leaning over a table, pondering something on a scroll, a lantern beside him.

I clomped over. "Captain?"

"Yeh," he replied, not looking up.

"My brother booked passage with you to the port city of Halabahna," I said.

"Cabins are that way. Got your names written in chalk on the door. Point out your trunks to my man there and we'll haul 'em up for you."

I shook my head, though he still hadn't looked up. "We can't go. I'm here to get our coin back."

"No refunds."

That hadn't occurred to me. I had no idea what to do. "Why not?"

Now he glanced at me, face crunched with irritation. "Could've sold your passage to someone else, couldn't I? We sail in two hours and who's going to show up at the last minute? I'm out money because you and your brother changed your minds." His voice went mocking on that last. "Fancy folk with your flighty ways. Sail with us or don't, but I'm keeping your coin." He returned his attention to the scroll on the table.

I had my pearls. If he didn't give me the coin, I'd have to use the pearl as passage on another ship. All he could do was say no again.

So I pulled the biggest one out of my pocket, holding it between him and the scroll, so it gleamed in the lantern light. I kept it pinched in my fingers, curled up to hide their feminine slimness. My nails were cracked and ragged from peeling off the glued-on shells and gems, so revealed little about my true origins.

It got his attention. Slowly straightening, he reached for it, but I pulled my hand back under my cloak.

"Who are you?" he asked, not demanding, like a guard might be, but curious.

"A man who wants his coin back."

"Is that so? If that pearl you showed me is real, it's worth ten times the coin ye paid."

Stupid me. Oh well. "But a pearl isn't as easy to spend."

"True. Let me see it then."

"So you can steal it from me? No."

He cracked a grin. "Look now, I'm a more or less honest man. If the pearl is real I'll give you your coin and then some, though I know that's not yours either, as we both know you're no man."

Abruptly fear hammered at me, my heart meeting it with furious harmony. And here I thought I'd done so well. The captain had me, and we both knew that, too. He held out a gnarled hand and I dropped the pearl in his palm.

He fingered it, then drew back his thick lips and ran it across his teeth, then grunted. Pocketing it, he reached under his coat, pulled out a leather bag and handed me the whole thing. "Still not what it's worth, but a sight more than the passage your 'brother' paid me. You'll need it."

I clutched it to my heart, willing the weight of coin to slow the frantic beating. "Thank you," I said.

"A piece of advice—don't let anyone see your hands. And no one else has pearls like that, Your Imperial Highness."

My voice choked. I could jump overboard. That was still an option.

"I won't tell your secret. I figure if you ran, you did it for good reason. But there's been Imperial Guard and one of your brothers come by the last several days asking if you booked passage."

Of course. Kral would have looked for ships going to Halabahna. Unforgivably stupid to have come here. But I did have coin now.

"If you're looking for another ship," the captain said, not unkindly now, "that one two slips over is heading out this morning to the Remus Isles. A lass can lose herself in those islands. And a queen runs the place. You might do well there."

"Thank you," I managed. I dug out another pearl, and offered it.

He folded a hand over mine, squeezing gently. "Keep it. The one could buy me a whole new ship and I just might do that, once we get to Halabahna. But keep those out of sight. I take it I shouldn't expect the fellow who booked the passage. I'm guessing his name isn't really Brian."

I laughed a little. Harlan had picked a name I might have guessed, had I been thinking clearly. "If he does come, and you can speak to him alone, tell him where I went. But don't tell anyone else."

He nodded, looking at his scroll again. "I'm not interested in giving up my newfound treasure and I don't kid myself that the high and mighty Imperial Prince wouldn't take it from me. I've never seen you and you'd think I'd recognize an Imperial Princess if one waltzed onto my ship, wouldn't I? Now get gone, lest you linger and get us both in trouble."

"Thank you," I said, one more time. Wishing I could say more.

He glanced at me and winked. "That's three times, which makes it magic. Good luck, Princess. Dasnaria will mourn losing you. Maybe you can come back someday."

Remembering my promise to Inga and Helva, I nodded.

"I will. I will come back. Someday."

~ Epigraph ~

I stood at the rail of the *Valeria*, watching the sun break over the ocean before us. Some other passengers stood at the rear of the ship, though many had dispersed, having waved goodbye to friends and family that had assembled on the docks and now diminished with distance. I wouldn't be so careless to be spotted there, but I couldn't make myself hide below.

The ship's sails billowed, creaking as the sailors cranked ropes to unfurl them, and with each new sail catching the wind, more water widened the distance between me and land.

A few slips down, Imperial carriages and armor glittered in the morning light. Crowds gathered round them, too, people pointing and sending up occasional cheers. I thought I spotted Kral's tall figure pacing the deck of the ship we'd been booked on, but I moved to the other side of the *Valeria*, just in case. I sorely wanted to see if I could spot Harlan, but I couldn't afford being sighted in return.

We were one among many ships heading out—a serendipity I hadn't thought to hope for. The one we'd been booked on—I'd never know the captain's name, and I wished I'd thought to ask—didn't look to be leaving any time soon. Imperial guards had spilled out, boarding other ships, hailing others to stand down, but the *Valeria* had already moved out. I'd heard the captain commenting acidly to his companion that the fucking Dasnarians weren't going to delay his schedule. We had a long, hard crossing ahead in winter as it was, and he wasn't losing a day to it.

The fucking Dasnarians. I rolled the phrase over in my mind, unsure of the meaning of the curse, but it sounded foul and I enjoyed it for that. One day I'd speak it aloud.

Taking one last look at the land of my birth, and of my imprisonment, I turned my back on it, facing resolutely forward. I gazed into the bright sun as long as I could, then dropped my eyes to the surging water. I even liked the shining gold red bubbles the scorching sun left in my vision after I looked away.

Through those blazing circles, animals leaped. Blue and gray like the water, one with the waves. Not elephants, of course, but kind of like them. Elephants of the water. I'd have to find out what they were really called.

A good omen. I smiled at them and lifted my face to the warming light. And sailed away into the sunrise.

The Lost Princess Chronicles continue in

Exile of Dasnaria

by

Jeffe Kennedy

In

Fall 2018.

Available at your favorite e-retailer!

Obey his command...

Master
of the
Opera

jeffe
kennedy

About the Author

Jeffe Kennedy is an award-winning author whose works include novels, non-fiction, poetry, and short fiction. She has been a Ucross Foundation Fellow, received the Wyoming Arts Council Fellowship for Poetry, and was awarded a Frank Nelson Doubleday Memorial Award.

Her award-winning fantasy romance trilogy *The Twelve Kingdoms* hit the shelves starting in May 2014. Book 1, *The Mark of the Tala*, received a starred Library Journal review and was nominated for the RT Book of the Year while the sequel, *The Tears of the Rose* received a Top Pick Gold and was nominated for the RT Reviewers' Choice Best Fantasy Romance of 2014. The third book, *The Talon of the Hawk*, won the RT Reviewers' Choice Best Fantasy Romance of 2015. Two more books followed in this world, beginning the spin-off series *The Uncharted Realms*. Book one in that series, *The Pages of the Mind*, has also been nominated for the RT Reviewer's Choice Best Fantasy Romance of 2016 and won RWA's 2017 RITA® Award. The second book, *The Edge of the Blade*, released December 27, 2016, and is a PRISM finalist, along with *The Pages of the Mind*. The next in the series, The Shift of the Tide, came out in August, 2017. A high fantasy trilogy taking place in *The Twelve Kingdoms* world is forthcoming from Rebel Base books in 2018.

She also introduced a new fantasy romance series, *Sorcerous Moons*, which includes *Lonen's War*, *Oria's Gambit*, *The Tides of Bàra*, and *The Forests of Dru*. She's begun releasing a new contemporary erotic romance series, *Missed Connections*, which started with *Last Dance* and continues in *With a Prince* and *Since Last Christmas*.

In 2019, St. Martins Press will release the first book, *The Orchid Throne*, in a new fantasy romance series, *The Forgotten Empires*.

Her other works include a number of fiction series: the fantasy romance novels of *A Covenant of Thorns*; the contemporary BDSM novellas of the *Facets of Passion*; an erotic contemporary serial novel, *Master of the Opera*; and the erotic romance trilogy, *Falling Under*, which includes *Going Under*, *Under His Touch* and *Under Contract*.

She lives in Santa Fe, New Mexico, with two Maine coon cats, plentiful free-range lizards and a very handsome Doctor of Oriental Medicine.

Jeffe can be found online at her website: JeffeKennedy.com, every Sunday at the popular SFF Seven blog, on Facebook, on Goodreads and pretty much constantly on Twitter @jeffekennedy. She is represented by Sarah Younger of Nancy Yost Literary Agency.

http://jeffekennedy.com
https://www.facebook.com/Author.Jeffe.Kennedy
https://twitter.com/jeffekennedy
https://www.goodreads.com/author/show/1014374.Jeffe_Kennedy

Printed in the United States
by Baker & Taylor Publisher Services